SUE BARTON – NEIGHBOURHOOD NURSE

Mona Stuart put her head in through the open car window. 'I want to talk to you about Cal, Mrs Barry. Your little girl said some things yesterday which gave me a pretty bad night. She thinks that Cal is unhappy, and that it's my fault. Do you think so?'

'Cal isn't unhappy in the exact sense of the word, Mrs Stuart. She's confused, and very much off on the wrong foot.'

'Is it my fault?'

Sue hesitated. 'My husband thinks it's tied up with her feeling that she's not important to you; that you don't love her.

Mona Stuart gave a faint gasp.

Sue Barton—
Neighbourhood Nurse

Helen Dore Boylston

KNIGHT BOOKS
Hodder and Stoughton

*The institution, the staff and the patients in this book are
entirely imaginary and bear no relation to any real
person or actual happening*

This book is sold subject to the condition that
it shall not, by way of trade or otherwise, be
lent, re-sold, hired out or otherwise circulated
without the publisher's prior consent in any
form of binding or cover other than that in
which this is published and without a similar
condition including this condition being
imposed on the subsequent purchaser.

Set, printed and bound in Great Britain for
Hodder and Stoughton Paperbacks, a
division of Hodder and Stoughton Ltd.,
Mill Road, Dunton Green, Sevenoaks,
Kent (Editorial Office: 47 Bedford
Square, London WC1 3DP) by
Cox & Wyman Ltd., Reading

ISBN 0 340 04009 2

Contents

To Margaret Ayer Cobb

I

Pure sentiment

THE hospital lay at the foot of the hill, its patterned lawns and giant elms walled in by red brick and granite in massive rectangles against the sky. The city's slums clattered and shrieked around it. An ambulance gong clamoured for right of way. Doctors' cars purred through the entrance gates – and so did a shiny new taxi which drew up before the wide stone steps of the Administration Building and deposited two young women.

They paid the driver and then, surprisingly, remained standing at the foot of the steps, looking up at the broad façade above them. Both wore fur coats – for the wind was raw – and small, gay hats. The taller of the two had an impertinent, tipped-up nose, dark brown hair, and high-arched eyebrows, which gave her face, even in repose, a look of amused inquiry. The other was slight and vivid, with delicate, clean-cut features, a warm skin, and copper-red hair which curled softly around her face. Her lively brown eyes regarded with interest the revolving door at the top of the steps.

'I hope,' she mused, 'that age has slowed that thing down. I'll never forget the first time I went through it – it practically hurled me into the rotunda, luggage and all.'

'You *would* remember something like that,' said her friend. 'I was so scared when I came that for all I know I may have gone in through the window. The first thing

I remember is standing in the Training School Office doorway with four supervisors looking at me.'

'Well, they looked at me, too – and then Ma Mason took me over to my room and was so nice I began to think I'd live. Let's go to the office first, Kit. If Miss Matthews is off duty we can come back afterwards.'

As they went up the steps Kit said, 'There's one thing about being an old grad – I'll bet all the head nurses and supervisors were probationers when we were here. We can intimidate them. Look out, Sue! For heaven's sake! Can't you manage that door *yet*?'

Her warning was unheard, for her friend had gone through the revolving door with such rapidity that it just missed snatching Kit's handbag from her hand. She waited, grumbling, until the door slowed.

Just inside was an Information Desk and telephone switchboard. The clerk at the desk looked up, saw two backs going through a glass door into a large, high-ceilinged rotunda, and called after them:

'Just a minute, please!'

The young woman with the copper-red hair turned, smiling, and said, 'It's all right. We're just going to the T.S.O.'

Her smile was disarming, but her use of the initials T.S.O. placed her at once as a nurse, and the clerk nodded.

The two continued on their way across the rotunda, and paused outside an open door which bore on its frosted-glass panel the word 'Principal'.

Miss Matthews, stout in her white uniform, was sitting at a roll-top desk bending over a spread of papers. Her broad, high-cheekboned face was intent and she did not look up until an apologetic knock penetrated her concentration.

'Come in,' she said. Then with a sudden, warm smile

she rose. 'Why, Katherine Van Dyke!' She caught a glimpse of red hair behind Kit. 'And Sue Barton! How nice to see you! Sit down and tell me what you're both doing.'

They found chairs and sat down, warmed by Miss Matthew's pleasure, and a little startled to see that her once-chestnut hair was now completely white.

Miss Matthews turned to Sue. 'Of course, you're Mrs Barry now – not Sue Barton. I have difficulty in remembering married names but I should remember yours. Dr Barry did such splendid work here. And I've heard very good things of you.'

'What?' said Sue, involuntarily.

Miss Matthews laughed. 'I mean the work you've done in New Hampshire in establishing a Rural Nursing Course in Public Health work in your hospital there. We're very proud of you. Are you still working?'

'Not very much,' Sue admitted. 'I relieve the visiting nurse from time to time, and do a good deal of neighbourhood first aid, and I can be called on in any emergency – but I have three young children and I honestly feel that it's a mother's business to look after her children herself. If I'm doing that, I can't –'

Miss Matthews caught the note of apology in Sue's voice.

'My dear girl,' she said. 'Bringing up children is a matter of the highest importance – as you have just pointed out. We're always delighted when we find our graduates using their training to its fullest advantage. An intelligent, skilled nurse has a great deal to give motherhood.'

Sue was fully aware of this, but hearing Miss Matthews say it was very pleasant. Ever since Sue had gone through the revolving door into the familiar atmosphere of the hospital, she had been feeling guilty and uncomfortable. So much had gone into her training – so much effort and knowledge. She had been taught science as new as the hour, and skills as old as compassion. What was she doing with them? Taking care of three children – probably doing it no better than any girl who could scrape through senior high. So she was comforted in thinking that she might be doing it better because of her training.

Miss Matthews turned to Kit. 'What about you, Miss Van Dyke?' she asked.

Kit grinned. 'I took over Sue's job as head of the nursing school when she resigned, but just now I'm having a leave of absence for the summer.'

'You're going home to Canada?'

'I am. And I'm not going to do a thing all summer except lie in a hammock with my feet up.'

'It sounds delightful,' said Miss Matthews wistfully. Then to Sue, 'Isn't Dr Barry superintendent of that hospital?'

'Oh yes. He has been, ever since it was built. I think he misses his regular practice – but I'm thankful. His hours are regular, you know, except for emergencies, and he has two interns now. I'm probably the only doctor's wife in the state who sees much of her husband.'

'I'm sure you're a great help to him,' Miss Matthews said.

'I don't know,' said Sue, considering this. 'I try to be, but the only thing I can do is a bit of co-ordinating work, once in a while.'

Miss Matthews, unaccustomed to small communities and small hospitals, and an absence of social service workers, looked puzzled.

'Co-ordinating?' she said.

Sue tried to explain. 'Well, for instance,' she said after

a moment, 'Bill is about to discharge a patient from the hospital this week – a young farmer named, of all things, Fred Button. His chest was crushed and he needs very light work, out of the weather, but with adequate pay – because he has a large family to support. A job like that is difficult to find in Springdale – in combination. So Bill wants me to cope with it, if I can. . . . I have more time to look around.'

'I see,' said Miss Matthews. 'I've always said that doctors should marry nurses. Not that a wife who wasn't a nurse couldn't help in a situation like that – but training makes a difference.'

'I suppose that's true,' Sue agreed, thinking, however, that her year in the Henry Street Visiting Nurse Service had made even more difference.

Miss Matthews talked with Kit for a few minutes about changes in nursing-schools, and then Kit glancing at Sue, raised her eyebrows.

Sue rose. 'We mustn't keep you, Miss Matthews,' she said. 'It's been awfully nice to see you. May we go around the hospital?'

Miss Matthews, too, had risen, and held out her hand. 'By all means,' she said. 'Especially the Children's Ward. It's been entirely rebuilt, and I'm sure you'll be interested.'

'Oh yes.'

Miss Matthews' office had seemed very hot, but the air of the rotunda was cool against their faces as they crossed it to follow a maze of corridors past X-ray rooms, Hydrotherapy, and various offices. They arrived at last in an immense, rectangular space of red brick and tiles, with great windows which looked out over the main hospital grounds.

'The Big Brick Corridor' was the point through which everyone must pass to go to the wards, the nurses' homes, the dining-rooms, the operating amphitheatre, the new buildings, and the old hospital.

Sue and Kit had crossed its red-rose floor a thousand times by day and by night. They had scurried over it as probationers, had moved grandly across it in their first caps, had marched through it to their graduation exercises. Now, uncertain, they paused in a slant of sunlight from one of the big windows.

'Where'll we go first?' Kit asked. 'Old, or New, or Amphitheatre?'

'Amphitheatre, don't you think? But let's just look around outside for a minute.'

They opened the door to the grounds and stepped outside. The lawn was just turning green with early spring, and the elms, they saw, were scarcely in bud. The Children's Ward, they knew, usually spent summer on the grounds, in tents, but Sue was not thinking of that now. She was looking at the old hospital – the original building – built over a hundred years ago.

It was a domed building of grey stone with ivied columns on either side of the wide central steps. Mats and fingers of ivy clung to the walls in a mist of budding green. It was a beautiful hospital, its lines flowing together in the harmony of utter simplicity. The massive buildings beside it, towering in stark modernity, could neither detract from it nor dwarf it.

Sue and Kit had seen it through the dimness of falling snow, through slanting rain, under clear autumn skies, and, as now, in the tender light of spring. They had tramped away more than one year of their training on its old floors.

'Funny how the place gets you,' Sue said at last. 'It's still in Dad's bones. And of course Bill is simply –'

'Heaven help your grandchildren!'

'You mean they'll have the place thrown at them from all sides? What a wonderful idea! Bill and I can chain them to our trembling old knees and tell them long, dull stories – all mixed up.'

She paused to look across the grounds. They were deserted, for the spring wind was too cold for patients to be out.

Kit glanced up idly, and then with interest, for Sue was staring tenderly at an empty intersection of gravel walks. An odd half-smile curved the corners of her mouth. 'Want me to get you a handful of gravel to take home?' Kit asked.

'I must have been half-witted,' Sue said, dreamily. 'And I'll never forget the chimes. The air was full of them.'

'Yes dear. Any voices? Or spots before your eyes?'

'Why no, I didn't –' Sue began seriously, and then turned on Kit. 'Oh, go jump in the lake!'

'Well, after all! You can't just leave me standing here while you go winging off on chimes in a half-witted condition.'

'Why can't I? But if you really want to know – right there is where Bill asked me to marry him – the night of the Christmas dance. I was simply freezing, too, and we'd had a row – oh, a very nice, well-bred one, in modulated voices. I thought the way he'd behaved with Eleanor Gerard was a little bit too much – and it was. And Bill was horribly stuffy about that bore, George Lamson. But – then we came out here and everything was all right.'

'Then why were you half-witted?'

'Because I didn't know whether I wanted to marry Bill or not.'

'Why you idiot!'

'That's what I said. Come on, we'd better go in.'

They closed the door carefully behind them and went

across The Big Brick Corridor to another, much darker, which they followed for a short distance. Then they pushed open a pair of brassbound, swinging doors.

They were confronted by a white-tiled rotunda in which was a solitary desk. Around it, in all directions, were doors to operating-rooms, or corridors leading to operating-rooms. They sniffed the familiar smell of ether and scorched cloth and smiled at the young supervisor who came forward to meet them.

'We're visiting alumnae,' they explained.

'Oh! Would you like me to take you round?'

They wanted to say that they had known this place inside and out when she was still playing hopscotch, but answered courteously that she needn't bother. 'We just stepped in for a moment,' Sue told her. 'Is anything going on, or are you all cleared up?'

'All but an exploratory laparotomy. Would you like to watch? I can get you gowns –'

'Oh no thanks. With our hats and high heels it seems rather complicated. Which room is it in?'

'The West room.'

'Well, we'll just skip it, and look in on the others for old times' sake.'

The young supervisor smiled. 'If there's anything I can do, just let me know,' she said.

They promised and wandered away, through the gleaming, hissing sterilizing-room, smiling as they listened to the talk of the nurses. They peered into the instrument room, all shining glass and glittering steel, drifted through the white perfection of deserted operating-rooms – and felt increasingly torn between their feeling of strangeness and their sense of belonging. Memories met them at every turn – but so did strange faces.

'I'm not so crazy about this,' Kit said gloomily. 'I feel

like last year's dead leaves. We might just look in on the new buildings.'

But the new buildings, though impressive, were too unfamiliar, and after a brief glance through one ward, they turned back to The Big Brick Corridor and the old hospital, where so much of their training had been spent. Here there were fewer changes, except for the kitchens which had once been tiny, hot and inconvenient, and were now spacious, cool, and highly efficient.

Young nurses in grey and white uniforms were courteous to them. Probationers stared. A blond intern in white sprang to open a door for them.

'Why, he's a baby,' Kit muttered to Sue when the door had closed again. 'They can't have been that young when we were here.'

'Don't kid yourself,' said Sue. 'They were twenty-four, but we were – eighteen. Let's go over to the Children's Ward. Miss Matthews said we'd be interested.'

They ignored the elevator to climb two long flights of stone stairs, but despite Miss Matthews' statement that the Children's Ward had been entirely rebuilt, they were startled when they opened the door.

The old ward had been one large room, lined with cribs and with fireplaces at each end. The floor had always been cluttered with aged toys, and the beds were always untidy from the scramblings of small patients.

The new ward consisted of two large rooms and a sun porch, in a much better state of order. There were shoulder-high glass partitions between the cribs; the walls were cream-coloured, and bright with Mother Goose murals; the equipment was new; the toys were delightful; the ward was air-conditioned. But the big, old-fashioned fireplaces were gone, and with them the rocking-chairs in which pain, homesickness, and bad dreams had been rocked away. The head nurse took Sue and Kit around, very proud of the ward, the kitchen, the laboratory, the beautiful, modern equipment. They had reached the older children's room, when Kit asked:

'What's happened to the fireplaces? I mean – it's obvious that they've been taken out – but why?'

'Because the chimneys were taken out of the wards below and above, so the fireplaces were useless. It's a shame, isn't it? They must have been fun, even if they were old-fashioned.'

Sue, standing among the cribs, missed Kit's reply. She was remembering how, at night, the ward intern used to sit before the fire, rocking and humming and telling stories while he held a pair of small feet in his large hand. The ward had been snug and warm and probably not at all well ventilated.

How young I was, Sue thought, and how many children I rocked to sleep here.

The baby voices and the creak of the rocking-chair came back to her through the remembered sound of rain and the smell of wood smoke.

The sudden lowering of the head nurse's voice caught Sue's attention and brought her back to the present. 'Umbilical hernia,' the head nurse murmured. 'Post-operative. He's been like that ever since he came. We've tried everything, but he won't respond or take an interest in anything – just lies there.'

Sue followed her glance to the corner of the ward where a boy of about six lay staring sullenly at the wall. Sue would like to have gone to him, but realized in time that this was not her ward. After a second of hesitation she trailed after Kit and the head nurse who had reached the doorway to the Babies' Ward and were standing there talking. Sue paused to smile at a flushed and restless five-year-old with a heavy cast on his leg. He returned her smile cheerfully, but his lips were dry from fever and he rubbed at them with the back of his hand. As she moved on, a young nurse came in with a glass of iced lemonade. The small boy clutched it with both hands and drank eagerly.

In the next partition was a little girl, lying face down, and Sue's heart gave a sudden leap. She forgot Kit, forgot the head nurse, forgot this was not her ward. She bent over the crib.

'What's the matter, darling?' she asked softly.

The child stirred and turned on her side. 'I want my mummy,' she said.

'I know you do. It's horrid to be away from her, isn't it?'

The child sat up. 'Are you a mummy?'

'I certainly am. I have a little girl of six, and two little boys – twins. They're four, and they have red hair.'

'Oh! I have a sister – bigger than me. What's your little girl's name?'

'Tabitha. What's yours?'

'Rosemary.'

'That's a lovely name. But do you know what? You look so much like Tabitha that I jumped when I saw you. She has dark hair and pigtails – just like yours. And she has the bluest eyes I ever saw – except yours – and I *think* –' Sue paused and laughed into the wide blue eyes – 'I think – yes – you have the same nice smile that she has too.'

'Did you go away and leave her in a hospital?'

Oh-oh! Sue thought, and prayed for inspiration. 'No,' she said at last. 'I've never left her in a hospital because she's never been sick. But if she *were* sick, very sick, I'd have to.'

'Why?'

'Because I'd want her to get well, and they don't let mummies stay in hospitals. There's nowhere for them to eat or sleep, and they'd get in the way of the nurses who are taking care of you. It's a *rule* that mummies can't stay. If they tried, the doctors would have to *make* them go home.'

Rosemary stared, silent.

The words, Sue realized, meant little to the desolate child whose feeling that she had been abandoned eclipsed everything else. Sue tried again.

'Rosemary,' she said, 'your mummy is feeling just the way you feel – all lonely and horrid and cross and wanting you more than anything.'

'How do you know?'

'Because I'm a mother too, and that's how *all* mothers feel. Shall I tell you what your mother is doing right now?'

Rosemary nodded, her eyes bright.

'Well, let's see. It's nearly five o'clock – so she'll be planning to start supper, and she'll be wondering what *you're* going to have, and hoping you'll like it, and she'll be wishing she could make it for you. She won't want to look at your place at the table because you're not there and that's going to make her feel like crying. And all the time she's putting things on the stove and taking them off again and setting the table and eating and doing the dishes she'll be trying to guess what you're doing.

'I expect if your daddy says something to her, or your sister asks for something, she'll say "What?" Because she won't be listening, you know – she'll have been thinking about you, and wondering if you're comfy.

'But no matter how lonely *she* is, she'll hope and hope that you aren't. And then when she goes to bed, the special part of her that belongs to you and no one else will *really* fly away here to you, loving you all night long. So you see, she hasn't really left you at all.'

'Is there really a special part of Mummy that belongs all to me?' Rosemary said, wondering, 'Could I *see* it?'

'No, you couldn't see it, but it'll be here just the same. And if you know it's here, you'll have a nice, warm, safe feeling – all the time.'

'Oh!' Rosemary breathed.

Sue leaned over to kiss her. It was not until she straightened up that she became aware of the intense silence in the room, and glanced around.

From every crib, she met wide, happy eyes. The five-year-old in the cast was no longer restless, and over in the corner the six-year-old boy was propped up on one elbow, his sullenness gone. The head nurse and Kit were standing motionless in the doorway.

Sue moved towards them, but when she reached the door she turned. 'Good-bye,' she said, to all the small faces. 'Eat great big suppers – and don't forget about tonight – *everybody*!'

'We won't!' arose in chorus.

'Come on, Kit,' Sue said, hurriedly. 'We've got to find some place to have dinner.'

'Well!' said the head nurse. 'That was really something! Thanks a lot! You know, Mrs Barry, *you* ought to be running a children's ward.'

'Heavens!' Kit said, opening the door into the hall. 'Don't suggest it! She's practically running one now – right in her own house.'

Sue grinned, stepped out into the hall, and said comfortably, 'But it's an old-fashioned one.'

2

Home again

THE midnight train began to move at last with a jerk which might have dislocated Sue's neck if she had been sitting up. Happily she was not sitting up, but lying comfortably in her berth. It had the usual green, cosy, back-to-the-cave quality of all train berths, and Sue had pried open the window and the porter had brought her another blanket, so she was neither suffocating nor freezing. She lay in thankful relaxation watching the lights outside picking up speed.

Kit's train had departed for Canada at eleven o'clock, and Sue had waved until it was out of sight – a performance which caused several people to stare at her. Then she retired to the station dining-room for an oyster stew, hoping it would make her sleepy. After two days with her father and mother who thought of her as sixteen, and today at the hospital where she felt eighteen, she needed a good night's sleep to restore her to maturity.

She finished the stew, picked up her bag, and went aboard the train, but even after she was settled in her berth her mind obstinately refused to detach itself from other days which seemed, just now, more real than the present.

It was all the fault of that infernal revolving door, she thought. It had hurried her straight back to her first day as a student nurse. She'd gone on from there – and was still going.

She wished she'd had time to go down into the honey-comb of passages under the hospital. There was just one place there which certainly belonged to her if it belonged to anybody.

She lay motionless, her hands clasped behind her head and her eyes fixed on a reflected point of light on the dark wall at her feet, but it was not the point of light she saw. Her mind's eye was looking at giant white pipes lining the walls and ceiling of the underground passage, and at the slim redheaded girl lost among them, and in a fine state of panic.

It was there that Bill had come upon her and had been charming and sympathetic. She saw him now as she had seen him then – a tall, broad-shouldered intern, all in white. He'd had no moustache then, and he'd stood with one hand against the wall looking down at her. There had been nothing to tell her that this was her first meeting with her future husband.

Three years later, on the day of her graduation from the hospital, and in that exact spot she had at last told him that she would marry him – if he'd wait until she had spent a year in the Henry Street Visiting Nurse Service.

He had agreed, poor darling. What else could he do?

Then there'd been Henry Street and the tiny, entire house she and Kit had been able to rent – because it was supposed to be haunted. It had been haunted all right. Sue laughed softly in the dim train berth, remembering the night she and Kit had waited, behind the couch in the tiny, moonlit living-room. They had waited and watched, paralysed, while the cellar door opened slowly – slowly.

That same winter was the one in which she'd had the frightful quarrel with Bill in a night club, and she'd stalked out of his life for ever.

What dopes we were, she thought. Both of us!

The Henry Street training had been wonderful, though. She'd worked on the East Side, in Chinatown, in Harlem, and all of it had brought her at last to Springdale, to work with Bill until they were married. It was all still vivid – the typhoid epidemic, the hurricane, Kit's coming, the Springdale hospital being built.

'How young I was!' she mused, and thought of her wedding-day, which had been more maddening and ludicrous than impressive – except for those few minutes when she was going up the aisle on her father's arm, her eyes on Bill's face, while he waited for her.

Again the sense of guilt she had experienced in the hospital seized her and she began to argue with herself. Certainly, she'd been very happy – was there anything wrong with that? She'd made Bill happy, too – she hoped – and this could hardly have been the case if she had devoted more time to nursing instead of to his home and children. It was absurd to think of herself as wasted! She wrenched her mind away from the stimulating activity of hospital life.

It would be wonderful to be home, Sue thought, curling deeper into the blankets, and as the train rocked on through the darkness her mind turned to her children. Vacations were all very well, but nothing could compensate for the absence of two small redheaded boys, and a little dark-haired girl with pigtails and a sweet mouth. How they would all have loved the train!

Sue thought about them in a sudden intensity of longing – the twins, redheaded, freckled, identical in looks, in movements, in their voices – but not in their interests. Johnny was her steady one, a carpenter and builder. Jerry was the restless one, always wandering and unsettled and usually in trouble. Tabitha had a thousand moods in a day – and a clear, disconcertingly logical mind.

She was a sensitive child, deeply loving, and often difficult.

Sue was beginning to feel drowsy when a sudden thought aroused her. This wretched train would get in at six in the morning. Poor Bill! She hoped he wouldn't get up for it. His face appeared before her with startling clarity – short black hair brushed straight back from his forehead, shapely head, deep-set clear blue eyes, short clipped moustache, firm mouth. She hoped he wouldn't try to meet her – but it would be very nice if he did.

He did – though not quite on time.

When Sue descended from the train at six the next morning there was no one in sight, and the train crept away and left her shivering despite her fur coat. Spring in the White Mountains is a cold season.

A door in the small, dingy station opened and a lank, overalled man peered out. 'H'a ya, Mrs Barry,' he drawled.

'Why, hello, Ezra. Mercy! This wind is like ice!'

'Dunno but 'tis, at that,' said Ezra cautiously. 'Been gone quite a spell, ain't you?'

'Only three days. Two with my mother and father, and one in Boston.'

'So? Well, the doctor, he telephoned to tell you he'd be right along. Better step inside. They's a stove in the waiting-room – if it ain't gone out. Haw! Haw!'

Sue had had previous acquaintance with the waiting-room.

'Thanks, Ezra,' she said, 'but I'll wait here if the doctor isn't too long.'

'Ayuh,' said Ezra and retired.

Sue's glance went beyond the platform to the neat white houses of Springdale clustered along the river bank all down the narrow valley. Prosperous farms dotted the slopes above, and beyond these the White Mountains ringed the horizon. The smell of their snow was sharp in the clear air and Sue drew a deep breath of enjoyment. Home! She walked twice to the end of the platform and back before the cold made her think with less revulsion of the waiting-room.

Then she heard a car door slam and an instant later Bill was dashing along the platform to envelop her in an immense hug.

'Why did you get up, darling?' she said against his shoulder. 'After all, I'm a big girl now and –'

'I had my reasons. Not, you understand, that I wanted to see you – but I thought it would make a change not to have all three kids in bed with me before I was fully awake. So I skipped out. When you're here it's not so bad. They –'

'Yes. They get in with me.'

'Sure. That's what you're for.' Arm in arm, laughing, they went around the end of the station to the car.

'How are they, Bill?'

'Great! Jerry has hugged a skunk; Johnny painted his eyelids with red nail polish, and Tabitha got stung by something she claims was the size of a house and made a noise like thunder.'

'Jerry hugged a skunk! Oh, Bill! How on earth –'

'It got into the empty garbage pail by the cellar door. Jerry got in with it and embraced it passionately.' Bill added, as an afterthought, 'He doesn't smell noticeably, *now.*'

'Thank goodness! Lordy, I'm glad to be home!'

'Lordy, I'm glad to have you!'

They drove out of the village in comfortable silence and turned up a winding mountain road.

'Veazie Ann all right?'

Sue had inquired more from affection than from any thought that Veazie Ann might not be all right; she had a substantial quality that seemed indestructible.

Veazie Ann Cooney was an old and valued friend, a native of Springdale, and long a widow. When Sue first came to Springdale she had rented a room in Veazie Ann's little house, and had not only enjoyed it but had come to depend on Veazie Ann's calm wisdom and unfailing humour. They had parted with mutual regret at the time of Sue's marriage. After Tabitha was born, and when the twins were on the way, Sue and Bill had moved from the small superintendent's cottage on the hospital grounds to their present, much larger house. Bill had insisted on Sue's having help of some kind, and they were looking for a maid when Veazie Ann suggested that she might do instead. She had worked for a time at the Information Desk at the hospital, but had long since retired.

'I might's well be with you folks,' she told Bill. 'I can rent my place easy, and I been kind of lonesome, home, with Sue gone. Besides, I like young ones and a man around the house.'

It turned out to be a perfect arrangement and Veazie Ann had been with them ever since, as much a part of the family as Sue, Bill, or the children. But Sue had stopped thinking of Veazie Ann; she was leaning forward, her eyes on the white house ahead.

The house was large, solidly square, well back from the road, and standing with dignity among its elms and maples. A lane edged with barberry bushes turned in beside it and meandered past a decorous line of out-buildings and a large red barn. To the left of the lane, opposite the barn, a rocky hill pasture tilted sharply upward against the sky.

The side lawn was cluttered with three swings, a

child's cart, a sand pile, and a slide, but the front lawn, though still brown from winter, was smooth and neat. The living-room windows looked out across it and the road into a blue space which concealed Springdale valley. Beyond, rising gradually from foothills, was the entire sweep of New Hampshire's Presidential Range. Mount Washington lifted a snow-covered head out of a scarf of clouds, and luminous shadows drifted across its scarred flanks.

Bill swung the car up the lane and stopped.

The back kitchen door was opened by a stout, elderly woman with a serene face and smiling eyes – Veazie Ann – and the children boiled out around her, followed by a waddling, stiff-jointed dachshund.

The twins flung themselves forward together, both yelling. Tabitha raced behind, very leggy, Sue realized. All their faces were ecstatic.

'Mummy! Mummy! Mummy!' they screamed, and behind them the fat dachshund moaned with excitement.

Sue disappeared in a welter of arms, legs, wet kisses, and a waving tail – to emerge dishevelled and misty-eyed.

'Did you bring us anything, Mummy?' Johnny demanded, and Tabitha and Jerry shrieked.

'Yes, I brought presents. Come on in the house.'

There was an album of gramophone records – by special request – for Jerry, a box of not-too-lethal tools for Johnny, and a toy cooking set for Tabitha. The children fell upon these with as much excitement as if they had never received a present before in all their lives. Each checked suspiciously to make sure that neither of the others had anything better, and then rushed off, one to the kitchen, one to the living-room, and one to the barn.

In the sudden quiet, Sue, Bill, and Veazie Ann sat down to breakfast.

Sue described her two days at home with her family, and her visit to the hospital, finishing with a description of the Children's Ward.

'Poor kids!' Bill said. 'Miss Matthews may be right about doctors marrying nurses, but if you ask me – all nurses ought to be mothers and all mothers ought to be nurses.'

'Ain't that kind of overdoing it?' Veazie Ann inquired, mildly. 'Kit get off all right?'

'Yes. It's going to be funny without her.'

'Are you telling me?' Bill said. 'I hope she's not going to get an impulse to resign – or get married – while she's up there. That Landers woman will do for the summer, but that's about all I can take of her.'

He rose. 'Well, I'd better get along to the hospital. I've got a nine o'clock rib resection.'

She went to the door with him, as always. He had kissed her good-bye and started down the steps when he halted suddenly and turned back.

'I darned near forgot to tell you,' he said. 'Miss Briscomb called up last night. Wanted to know whether you'd be at home this afternoon around two. You will, won't you?'

'Why, yes. I suppose so. What did she want?'

'Search me. But I thought you might tackle her about a job for Fred Button.'

'A job for Fred – oh! You mean in her greenhouses? But Bill – she's impossible! I haven't the faintest idea how to handle her.'

'Better you than me,' said Bill cheerfully, and went on down the steps.

3

Helpmeet

SUE was not, as a rule, a forgetful person, and she was quite as worried about Fred Button as Bill was, particularly because of Fred's children who were running wild while Mrs Button tried to earn enough to feed them. Miss Briscomb would be a problem, and Sue intended to give the matter serious thought. The trouble was that in the course of the morning's work she completely forgot that Miss Briscomb was coming.

For one thing, it was Sue's first day at home after a four-day absence; for another, Veazie Ann had started a thorough, old-fashioned house-cleaning. Sue wanted to turn out all the cupboards before Veazie Ann got to them. Tabitha, whose legs seemed to be getting longer by the minute, had to have two of her dresses let down before she went back to school from her spring vacation. The family's summer clothes ought to be brought down from the attic and hung out-of-doors, and this was a good day for it. Sue found a pair of Bill's gardening trousers on the floor, and received the immediate impression that not only had Bill, also, hugged the skunk, but that he had been rolling in compost and bone meal. She removed the trousers with a thumb and forefinger and hurriedly put them through the washing-machine. The children excited by their mother's return, called to her a dozen times an hour to admire what they had done, were doing, or planned to do. There was lunch to get, for Veazie Ann was too busy to attend to it.

After lunch Sue got the twins settled upstairs for their naps. Tabitha, too old for naps, was seized with a desire to play in the attic, and retired with four dolls and Maxl, the dachshund.

This, Sue thought, would be the perfect time to give the porch chairs a fresh coat of paint. The lunch dishes could wait.

Sue enjoyed painting and worked happily, humming to herself because she was glad to be home again. She wondered whether she would be enjoying herself so much if she didn't feel that she were playing truant from her uniform? She stepped back and looked defiantly at a chair – defiantly, and with satisfaction. There was a fresh breeze now, sweeping up from the valley. The chairs would dry quickly. A huge moving van passed, struggling up the grade, probably going to the old Irwin place which had been bought by a very famous artist, a woman named Mona Stuart.

Sue had never seen any of Mona Stuart's work and knew nothing about her, except such rumours as Veazie Ann brought home. Now the woman would be a near neighbour. Sue was wondering about her idly when she became aware of a long, glittering limousine turning up the lane.

The next moment she had hurled her paintbrush into a can of turpentine and was flying up the stairs to the guest room, where Veazie Ann was washing woodwork.

'Veazie Ann!' she called. 'Veazie Ann! Quick!'

'Land, Sue! What's the matter?'

'Plenty! Miss Briscomb's here! I forgot all about her! Oh, Veazie Ann, I can't see her yet! I look frightful! And I've got to get her to give Fred Button a job!'

'She won't, and you know it.'

'Maybe – but I can try. What have I got to lose?'

'Your circulation, most likely. She'll freeze it solid.

You want I should fix tea? It might warm her up some.'

'Oh, yes. Thanks.'

Veazie Ann was half-way down the front stairs when the knocker sounded. Sue, meanwhile, fled to the bathroom, peeling off her sweater, dabbed frantically at the paint on her face, and dashed to her room. She kicked off her slacks, scrambled into a housecoat, and raked a comb through her hair, trying, as she hurried, to think of a sure-fire line of attack which would get Fred Button a job. It didn't look hopeful.

Miss Briscomb was immensely wealthy. She had come to Springdale some years before as a summer visitor, had bought a large estate above the village, and now lived there the year round, absorbed by her gardens and greenhouses. She took an interest in local charities and gave to them liberally, but she had never been known to do anything for an individual case, and her manner discouraged everybody.

She was a tall, stately woman in her forties, with dark hair and eyes, a thin face, and a low voice. She seldom smiled, or altered her expression of calm detachment, and nobody knew what she was thinking.

Sue went downstairs, still undecided about the proper method of approach, and found Miss Briscomb standing by the living-room window which looked out across the valley. The tall figure turned, unsmiling as always, and held out her hand.

'How do you do, Mrs Barry. I hope this is not an intrusion.'

'No, indeed. I'm delighted. Won't you sit down?'

'Thank you. You have a beautiful view from here.'

'Yes, we have. You know, Bill and I wanted this house the first time we saw it, and all the time we were living in the superintendent's house at the hospital we were scared to death that somebody would buy this place. I thought we'd never get it. But after the children came along we really needed a larger –' Sue was chattering and she knew it, but anything was better than Miss Briscomb's awful formality.

Miss Briscomb sat down with her customary composure. Sue, who was not at all composed, took the opposite chair, wondering how anyone could be so consistently dead-pan.

Miss Briscomb proceeded to business at once. She had come to ask Sue about the new school which the town proposed to build. Why was it necessary, how much would it cost, and didn't this mean a large increase in the tax rate?

Sue explained about the school in detail, thankful to have a definite topic of conversation.

Miss Briscomb listened without comment, and continued to say nothing, though she nodded amiably when Veazie Ann brought in the tea tray. Sue poured tea and passed sandwiches and listened to her own voice carrying on what seemed to be an interminable monologue. Miss Briscomb interrupted it at last.

'Would you consider this expenditure necessary if you had no children of your own?'

'Certainly.'

'Are you sure? I'd like an unprejudiced opinion.'

Sue resisted an impulse to say 'Go soak your head.' Instead she replied carefully, 'I'm afraid I can't prove that my opinion is unprejudiced. You'll have just to accept my word that it is.'

'Quite,' said Miss Briscomb, and the conversation languished.

It was then that Sue decided to tackle the problem of the Buttons and get it over, regardless.

'Miss Briscomb,' she began. 'I'd like to talk to you about a patient who is being discharged from the hospital – a young farmer whose chest was crushed last autumn in a landslide. He's not going to be able to do farm work for some time – in fact, he can't do any heavy work – and he has a wife and four children. His wife has been supporting the children all winter by going out cleaning, and she's had to leave them alone a good deal. They *were* nice children, but she can't look after them this way, and they're going from bad to worse – dirty, ragged, mischievous. It's beginning to be serious mischief for the oldest boy. He's been caught stealing twice now. If their mother could stay at home she'd straighten them out. She's a good mother.'

'Why are you telling me all this, Mrs Barry?'

'Because I hope that you'll give Fred Button a job in your greenhouse – as soon as possible after he gets out of hospital.'

'Why should I?' Miss Briscomb's tone was one of mild inquiry – nothing else.

'For one thing, because he's an excellent gardener. For another – so that he can support his family and his wife can attend to his home. Greenhouse work is about the only thing Fred could do, right now. He's going to have to be careful for some time.'

'Then why doesn't *he* stay at home and look after the children?'

'Because,' said Sue patiently, 'his wife doesn't make enough to feed another mouth, and because the children need a decent home, constant supervision, patient understanding and a great deal of love.'

'I fail to see,' Miss Briscomb said, 'why their father shouldn't provide all that.'

'He could only do it in a general sort of way. A man

isn't equipped by nature to spend all his energies out-thinking children twenty-four hours a day. Besides he hasn't the continued experience.'

There was a pause. Then Miss Briscomb said calmly, her face devoid of expression, 'I haven't a place at present, but if I do I'll let you know.'

'Couldn't you make a place?'

'I'm sorry to disappoint you, Mrs Barry, but I can't feel that the situation warrants my putting a workman I don't need on my payroll.'

'I'm sorry too. The Button children are not bad children, and having a proper home again would make all the difference.'

Perhaps it was Sue's persistence, perhaps her words had more effect than she knew, but whatever the cause, Miss Briscomb seemed, for the first time, to hesitate. At that moment Tabitha's voice came down the stairs.

'Mummy, the boys are awake. May we come down?'

Sue snatched at a new possibility. If Miss Briscomb were really weakening, the appearance of healthy, happy children, rosy from their nap, clean, innocently rumpled and charming, might be more effective than any argument. Let her see children with the advantages she was denying the Buttons.

'All right,' she called to Tabitha, and then, to Miss Briscomb, 'I hope you don't mind, for a few minutes.'

'Not at all,' said Miss Briscomb, faintly, as the children clattered down the stairs. The twins went through the hall to the kitchen for their milk, but Tabitha came briskly into the living-room.

Sue gasped.

Tabitha's face was dirtier than her mother had ever seen it – which was saying a good deal. Her hands were even worse. One plait had come undone and her hair dangled stringily against her cheek. There was a rent in the knee of her overalls, revealing grimy pink skin.

'How do you do,' Tabitha said cheerfully to Miss Briscomb. 'I've been up in the attic. It was absolutely *filthy*! May I have a sandwich, Mummy?'

Sue found her voice. 'No,' she said. 'Not until you have washed your face and hands and changed your overalls. And ask Veazie Ann to plait your hair before you come back.'

Tabitha was ordinarily a co-operative and well-mannered child, but she took this occasion to whine. 'Oh, Mummy, *why* can't I have a sandwich now? I'm hungry.'

'You're also dirty. Do as I tell you, darling, like a good girl.'

Tabitha burst into tears and departed, dawdling in loud misery in the hall.

Sue would have preferred to ignore the entire matter, but felt that she had to say something. 'I assure you,' she said, 'that this is not the way my daughter usually looks or behaves. She –'

Whatever Sue had been about to say was lost in pandemonium as Johnny shot, yelling, into the living-room. His shoes were untied, and he had a milk moustache, and he was pursued by a conspicuously unbuttoned Jerry screaming, 'Stop thief! Stop thief!'

Both children were too excited to be aware of their mother or Miss Briscomb. They raced through the room and out the door, leaving an overturned chair behind them.

Sue rose with grim intent, and Miss Briscomb inquired – too gently, 'What is it, Mrs Barry? Has one of *your* little boys stolen something?'

Sue managed a hollow laugh. 'No,' she said, 'they're

just playing Peter Rabbit and Mr McGregor. If you'll just excuse me a moment –'

She had no difficulty in locating the twins. They were wrestling on the dining-room floor, and the din, Sue felt, could be heard for miles. Sue pulled them to their feet.

'Johnny! Jerry! Be quiet a moment and listen to me. I have a guest, and you are not to tear through the house like that. If you must play Peter Rabbit, go outdoors.'

They stared at her, crestfallen. 'I'm sorry, Mummy,' Jerry said, and Johnny added, 'We didn't mean to.'

Sue's heart melted. 'I know you didn't, darlings, but please *do* be quiet for a little while.'

'Can we see the guest?' Johnny asked, in the manner of one asking to be taken to the zoo.

Sue hesitated. The advantages of their good home were strikingly unapparent at the moment, but that was no reason for banishing them, poor babies. She retrieved Johnny's shoe from beneath the table, helped him to put it on, buttoned Jerry, and led them, one by each hand, to the living-room.

They smiled at Miss Briscomb, who produced a vague, brittle grimace in return, but she seemed unable to think of anything to say, and Sue made conversation and spread jam on bread simultaneously.

The twins were docile, and they tried earnestly to be quiet, but two small boys, just awakened from a long, refreshing nap are frantic with energy. Despite their efforts they trampled and squirmed, and Jerry hummed incessantly, beating time on the tea tray until Sue closed her fingers gently over his hand. Then he wandered away in search of other amusement, while Johnny leaned on the arm of Miss Briscomb's chair, and settled himself for a pro-longed fit of staring. Sue had just reached out to draw him away when a blast of organ music rattled the teacups.

'SILENT NIGHT! HOLY NIGHT!' roared the gramophone.

Miss Briscomb started violently, and Johnny dropped his bread, jam side down, on her sleeve.

'Oh, Miss Briscomb!' Sue cried. 'I'm so sorry! Let me –'

She was drowned out. '*ALL* IS CALM. *ALL* IS BRIGHT.'

'Jerry!' Sue shouted. 'Turn that thing off this *minute*!'

The gramophone gave a final earsplitting scream.

'HEAVENLY PEA – EECE,' it screeched, and was silent.

Sue tried to fix both boys with her eye. 'Jerry, I want you and Johnny to go out-of-doors and play. Scoot along. *Now!*'

She turned to Miss Briscomb who was dabbing at the jam on her sleeve, and said, desperately, 'Please let me do that. Oh, your hands too! Won't you come upstairs to the bathroom?'

Miss Briscomb wasted no words on polite protest. She rose at once, and the unhappy Sue led the way upstairs feeling that she was leading a funeral procession for Fred Button's last chance. After this exhibition of what having a mother around does *not* do for children, Miss Briscomb would be crazy if she thought it worth while to keep Mrs Button at home.

They met Tabitha in the hall, clean and shining, now that it was too late.

'Are you going to the bathroom, Mummy?' she asked. 'Why didn't you go to the downstairs one? Oh, I know – the towels are dirty.' She looked at Miss Briscomb.

'You know,' Tabitha said, 'this bathroom's awful old. The drain is terrible. My daddy thinks there's a dead dinnersaw in it.'

'A *what*?' said Miss Briscomb, startled into speech.

'A dinosaur,' Sue explained, feebly.

'Oh!'

She opened the bathroom door and stopped short.

'*Tabitha!*' she called in a strangled voice, backing up against Miss Briscomb. 'What is *this*?'

Tabitha pushed through. 'Oh,' she said, 'that's Johnny's dead mouse's bed. I guess he forgot to take it when he woke up. It smells, doesn't it?'

'Take it out, *please*, and put it in the incinerator.'

Tabitha emerged from the bathroom, bearing a doll's bed with a tiny pillow, upon which rested the dilapidated head of a long-deceased mouse. A clean wash-cloth, as a coverlet, was drawn up to the mouse's chin. The unconcerned Tabitha carried the bed and its contents down the hall in an almost visible odour of putrefaction.

Sue flung open the bathroom door, but her further apologies were never spoken, for Miss Briscomb was shaking with silent laughter.

After a stunned moment, Sue's own laughter rang out. She handed Miss Briscomb a towel, and Miss Briscomb retired, choking a little.

Sue waited at the head of the stairs. She felt better. Despite poor Fred, it was something to have made Miss Briscomb laugh.

Sounds of running water came from the bathroom, and muffled stirrings. Once Sue thought she heard hummings, and listened intently. Yes, Miss Briscomb *was* humming, humming a tune Sue felt she would remember for the rest of her life, even if she never heard it again.

'Si-lent night, Ho-oly night –'

It broke off abruptly in a kind of choke. Then the door opened and Miss Briscomb came down the hall, her face grave as usual.

'I'm afraid I must be going,' she said. 'It's getting quite late. I didn't realize –'

They went down the stairs together in silence; Miss Briscomb collected her gloves and bag, and Sue went to the door with her. On the step, Miss Briscomb paused.

'You may tell your Mr Button,' she said, 'to come to work whenever he is ready.'

She stared at her, feeling like the village idiot.

'I – I'm so glad,' she stammered. 'I mean – at least – I don't understand.'

'Well,' said Miss Briscomb, 'now that I have seen what children can do in a brief period of normal activity, I perceive that you were correct. They need someone to out-think them. I have known many brilliant men – leaders in their fields – but I cannot think of one who would be equal to a task of that proportion. A mother is a necessity.'

Thoughtfully she pulled on her white kid gloves.

'This has been a very entertaining afternoon. I hope you and your husband will dine with me sometime.'

'We'd love to,' Sue replied sincerely, and Miss Briscomb departed – tall, stately – and smiling.

Sue looked after her.

Well, she thought, I've been a help to my husband, all right. Only somehow I doubt if this is the way Miss Matthews pictures it.

4

Cal

SPRING can advance very rapidly in a week. The afternoon
was warm and the air smelled pleasantly of green grass
and brush fires. Midges jigged here and there in sociable
clouds, for bug season was beginning and it was time to
remove storm windows and put on screens. The storm
windows, in fact, were already off, and the last was dis-
appearing in the direction of the barn – balanced on Bill's
head. His tall figure moved briskly over the soggy ground,
happy in the freedom of blue jeans and an old flannel shirt.
If a smell of ether still clung about him he was not aware
of it, and wouldn't have cared anyway. This was Satur-
day, he was off duty for the afternoon, Sue was at home
again, and his only concern, at the moment, was the size-
to-be of his kitchen garden. He whistled as he went into
the barn, stacked the window in a corner with the rest,
and turned to encounter Johnny in a state of partial
undress.

'Daddy, my pants are falling off.'

His father grinned. 'So I see. Where's the button?'

'It fell down the hay chute.'

'Well, that could slow you up. You'd better go in to
your mother – Oops! Here – grab hold of them!'

'Wait a minute,' said Jerry's voice from the gloom of a
box stall. 'I've got the button, Daddy. It was right here.'
He emerged, pleased with himself, and departed with
Johnny for the house, where Sue, laughing, got out her

sewing-basket and sat down in the living-room with Johnny standing before her, ready for operations. Jerry watched for a few moments and then began to fidget.

'Mummy,' he said, 'I have to go to the bath-a-room.'

'Well, go along then,' Sue suggested, her head still bent over Johnny's button.

Jerry went away and she could hear him plodding up the stairs with the thunderous tread of the four-year-old. Once upstairs, however, his footsteps pounded absently on – past the bathroom – his errand forgotten for some new interest.

A voice spoke from the kitchen – Veazie Ann's. 'Tabs!' it said. 'Land of goodness, child, do stand from under!'

Sue heard the sticky, irreparable smash of an egg falling to the floor.

'There now!' said Veazie Ann.

'Oh!' Tabitha's voice was thin with distress. 'Oh, Veazie Ann, I *didn't* mean to joggle you!'

Her face, Sue knew, would have lost all its happy colour, and Veazie Ann would melt at once. She did.

'There! There! 'Tain't the end of the world. We'll get another egg and you can beat it. Come along in the pantry and pick out a nice big one.' Their steps went across the floor. The pantry door opened and slammed shut.

It was then that Jerry screamed.

Sue shot to her feet, leaving Johnny with the needle dangling from the button, and was racing up the stairs when Bill's yell reached her.

'SUE! UPSTAIRS HALL! QUICK!'

She didn't need the directions. She could see the open window at the end of the hall, with the screen against the wall beside it, and was running, had reached it, was climbing out, her eyes on Jerry's head and shoulders at the edge of the back-porch roof. He was clinging to a bracket which held up the gutter. One pudgy knee was hooked over the gutter trough; the other leg dangled in space – over a fifteen foot drop to the stone steps below.

'Hold tight, Jerry. Mummy's coming,' said Sue steadily.

The pitch of the roof was not steep but the warm shingles were damp and steamy under her hands, and her foot slipped with her first atttempt to put her weight on it. She sat quickly and began to hitch down the roof. The pounding of her heart shook her, and her eyes stung, seeing the terror in Jerry's little face. The treacherous shingles slid greasily upward beneath her.

'Bill!' she called. 'Where are you?'

'Right under him. I'll catch him if he falls – don't worry.'

Jerry's bright head was very close now and his agonized eyes were fixed on her face. She stretched herself flat and seized his shoulder and one arm. He burst into tears, his head against her cheek.

'There, darling, there! It's all right now!'

She peered over and tried to smile at Bill, whose face was as white as her own.

'Don't try to pull him back up,' Bill warned. 'That gutter isn't very strong. If it gives way, you'll both go over. Can you hang on to him while I get the ladder?'

'Of course I can, but hurry!'

Bill dashed away without a word.

'Mummy,' Jerry whimpered. 'I'm cold.'

It was shock, naturally. 'I know, dear, but it'll only be a minute.'

Johnny spoke suddenly from the window behind her. 'Oh!' he cried, pleased. 'Can I come out, too, Mummy?'

'No!' said Sue in her most awe-inspiring voice. Then

to Jerry, 'Don't move, darling. You must keep very still until Daddy comes.'

'Mummy,' Johnny persisted from the window. '*Why* can't I come out? Jerry is.'

'No, Johnny. I'll explain later. *Jerry!* Never mind about Johnny! You *must* keep still!'

There was a short silence. Sue's hands were beginning to ache. Where was Bill?

'I'm so tired. And you're hurting my shoulder,' Jerry wailed.

Sue changed her grip as best she could, and looked uneasily at the bracket holding the gutter. *The screws were weakening!*

Oh, Lord, Sue thought wildly, what'll I do? There must be *some* way to work this so he'll be safe, even if the gutter goes.

She poked cautiously behind her with her feet, hoping for a toe-hold, but there was nothing, and she had no way of moving higher up the roof without letting go of Jerry. She lay motionless, her eyes on the bracket. Jerry's face was pressed against her neck. What *was* Bill doing?

'Can I help?' inquired a voice from below.

Sue tore her eyes away from the bracket for a split second, and saw, standing on the lawn below, a girl of about fourteen. Sue had no idea who the girl was, but she might be adequate as a cushion for Jerry – if he fell.

'Stand on the steps,' Sue told her, 'and try to catch him if the gutter breaks. My husband has gone for a ladder. He'll be here in just a second.'

Jerry craned his neck and the gutter gave an ominous crack.

'*Stop that*, Jerry!' said Sue frantically, and tightened her grip.

Johnny bellowed from the window, 'I want to come out!'

Sue raised her voice but her eyes remained on the bracket screws. They were a little farther out now. 'Johnny,' she said, 'if you don't go downstairs at once, and stay there, I am going to take away your carpentry set for *five days*!'

It was in the shocked silence following this statement that Bill appeared with the ladder, which he set up with only a brief glance at the newcomer.

'Are you all right?' he demanded as his head came up level with Sue's and he took a firm grip on Jerry.

She flexed her aching hands. 'Of course, I'm all right. Do get him down, Bill, please.'

'Jerry, let go of Mummy's sleeve.'

Jerry clung to Bill, terrified at first, and then, as they began to go down the ladder, he brightened. Once on the ground he stared at the girl, who had been watching the proceedings, fascinated.

'What's your name?' said Jerry.

'Caroline Stuart. But everybody calls me Cal.'

'Well, I'm Jerry,' said Jerry, and turned a proud somersault.

'Not much the matter there,' said Bill, half to himself and half to Sue.

But Sue, watching the little boy so happily showing off, discovered that she was trembling, and scrambled hurriedly down the ladder. She clasped Bill's hand tightly when he reached out to help her.

'Hey!' he said, putting his arm around her. 'It's all over!'

'I know. I'm just having a delayed reaction. What do we do with Jerry? My impulse, now he's safe, is to do something drastic.'

'Well, he's had quite a scare. Bawl him out, and make him shut the window. He can do it – and I'll bet a nickel he won't climb out again. Don't worry – I'll put the screen on – *now*.'

'All right – and please put the ladder away before Johnny decides to go up and see where Jerry was.' She turned to the girl, who was obviously waiting to be invited in, and said, 'Won't you come in?'

'Thank you very much,' said the girl, promptly. 'I'd love to. But I wish you'd call me Cal.'

'Fine. Come in, Cal,' said Sue, really looking at her for the first time.

Goodness, she thought, for the child was startlingly beautiful, despite slacks and a brief, shapeless jacket. Her shining, honey-coloured hair hung to her shoulders, framing an exquisite face, with grey-green slanting eyes shaded by thick, dark lashes.

Jerry, who was staring at Cal in desperate admiration, said cheerfully, '*I* was on the roof!' It was an open boast and at the thought of those minutes over the gutter, Sue's temper exploded.

'Gerald Barton Barry!' she said. 'There was nothing smart about what you did! It was the naughtiest thing you've *ever* done! You've been told and told not to even play near an open window, and if you ever do it again I'm going to spank you with the *back of a hairbrush*! Do you understand?'

Jerry had turned his head away and he drooped conspicuously.

'Yes, Mummy,' he said faintly.

'Very well! When we get in the house you are to go up and shut that window – and come straight back down again!'

'All right, Mummy. I – I'm sorry.'

'You'd better be! Come on!'

They were met at the kitchen door by Johnny, and Cal stared from him to Jerry, her mouth open. 'My goodness!' she said, recovering. 'Twins! What fun! But how do you tell them apart, Mrs Barry?'

'I don't know,' Sue admitted, shooing the little boys before her into the kitchen and wondering how Cal knew her name. 'It's an acquired skill. Do take your things off, Cal, and let's all have something to eat. Jerry, go right up and shut that window – and *don't go anywhere else*! Come in the living-room, Cal. No – this way.'

They sat down in the bright, chintz-curtained living-room just as Tabitha appeared in the doorway. 'We've been down the cellar,' she began importantly, 'to get some apple butter to go with the –' she broke off to stare at Cal.

'Well, Mummy and *Jerry* have been on the roof,' Johnny returned, still outraged at not having been there himself.

'Why were you, Mummy?' Tabitha asked.

'Because Jerry climbed out and almost fell off,' Sue told her. 'Tabs, this is Cal.'

Cal smiled at Tabitha from the depths of her armchair and Johnny, catching the smile, said abruptly. 'You're pretty, Cal.'

The smile faded instantly. 'You know what?' she said to Johnny. 'I can make nice boats that really sail, and I can tie knots, too. I'll show you sometime.'

But Johnny ignored the boats and knots. 'You're awful pretty,' he insisted.

Cal turned away from him, her expression so sulky that Sue was startled. After a moment, Sue arose and retired to the kitchen. Refreshments might be helpful at this point. What on earth ailed the child? Most girls, by the time they're fourteen, are in an agony of doubt about their looks, but Cal's beauty was so striking that she couldn't possibly have any doubts about it. So what was wrong? Why the sullen resentment?

When Sue returned from the kitchen bearing a tray laden with glasses of milk and a plate of Veazie Ann's gingerbread, hot from the oven, Jerry was back downstairs. Cal was cheerful again, and was telling the children a story. They attacked the gingerbread and milk with their usual hearty enthusiasm. Cal's appetite was equally healthy, and the story was abandoned.

Sue helped herself to a piece of gingerbread and sat down to enjoy the picture made by Cal's vivid young beauty surrounded by the charms of the Barry children.

'I've never been in the White Mountains before,' Cal said at last, sitting back, replete. 'They're lovely.'

Sue agreed, and then, her curiosity getting the better of her, asked if Cal were visiting the neighbourhood.

'Oh, no! We've come to live here – in that white house up the road – the one with the willows.'

'But that's the old Irwin place.'

Cal nodded. 'That's right. Mother's bought it.'

'But – then your mother must be the artist – Mona Stuart?' Sue was astonished. She had heard that Mona Stuart was middle-aged and that her husband was dead, but there had been no mention of a daughter.

'I didn't realize –' Sue began, and then stopped.

'You mean you didn't know about me?' Cal laughed. 'I suppose Mother forgot to mention me. She usually does.'

There seemed nothing to say in reply to this, and Sue remarked that the old Irwin place was very lovely.

'Yes, it is. Mother didn't do anything to the house, but she's made the barn over into a studio. I'm so glad you're our neighbours. I think doctors and nurses are so *glamorous*!'

Sue laughed. 'How did you know I was a nurse?'

'Oh, it was Mr Phinney, who sold Mother the house. She wanted to know who lived near, because she doesn't like to be bothered, you know, even when she's not working. So Mr Phinney said nobody lived near except Doctor and Mrs Barry, and Mrs Barry used to be a nurse, and you were nice people. And Mother said she didn't care what you were as long as you didn't come around and pester her. She meant because she's famous – people are awful sometimes. And Mr Phinney said, "Madam, nobody around here's going to be interested if you're ring-straked and speckled! You tend to your own business and we'll tend to ourn. If you can't get along with your neighbours you'd better buy somewheres else." Mother laughed and laughed, afterwards. She was tickled to death, and she told Cornelia all about it.'

Sue grinned. Lot Phinney, the town's first selectman, was not noted for patience and forbearance, especially with city people.

'Anyway,' Cal went on, 'when Cornelia told me about you I wanted to come over and meet you.' She paused and then added strangely. 'I knew it would be all right because doctors and nurses are different. They're usually thinking about *important* things.'

Sue could make nothing of this cryptic remark, so she let it pass, and inquired, 'Who is Cornelia?'

'Oh, she's Mother's maid. She used to be my nurse when I was little and –'

She was interrupted by Jerry, who had been quiet as long as he could and now came to lean on the arm of Cal's chair. 'I'm glad you're going to live here,' he said.

Cal's face lighted. 'Are you? Then I'm glad too.'

'I like to look at you,' Jerry said.

'Oh,' said Cal flatly.

Sue hesitated and then asked gently, 'Do you mind being pretty, Cal?'

Cal's lower lip trembled. She drew a long quavering breath and burst out, 'Yes, I do! I *hate* it! It's like a curse on me!'

'But that's too bad, Cal. Most people would love to look like you. Why do you hate it?'

'Because nobody cares if I'm nice – or fun – or helpful – or interesting – or *anything*! I'm just flesh tints and line and colour! I'm not a person at all!'

'But Cal,' said Sue, one eye on her startled children, 'I'm sure that's not really true. It couldn't be! Do you pose for your mother?'

'Not any more. She says she got all of me when she did her "Girl with Catkins". And that's another thing people think about instead of me – even the girls at school. I'm just a model. And the girls didn't like me.'

'Are you sure they didn't like you?'

'Of course I am! When we were in Mexico I got along all right in school, but then we came to New York, and Mother didn't know what to do with me, and a friend told her to send me to Fenchley, and she did, and it was *awful*!'

'What happened, Cal?'

'Oh, they wouldn't ask me to be in anything, and they used to laugh at me. I heard them, all right. They used to call me "Glamour Puss!" I *hate* girls!'

Sue knew about Fenchley – a fashionable New York school attended by precocious children of the very rich. They would feel an automatic hostility to any outsider, and, resenting Cal's beauty, would find it a convenient weapon for ridicule – the poor kid!

'What about boys?' Sue asked.

Cal looked up with as much surprise as if Sue had asked, 'What about unicorns?' and said, 'I've only met a few boys at some of the parties Cornelia made me go to. They just stare and act silly. They aren't any fun.'

Sue laughed. 'You certainly *don't* know much about boys. You may be surprised. Are you going to school here next winter?'

'I suppose so,' drearily, 'but it'll be just the same.'

'But it won't, Cal. This is a resort centre, and the young people here are used to meeting all kinds of strangers. They aren't going to turn inside out at the sight of a new girl. They haven't time. They have to help out at home, and attend to business in school. If you're friendly they'll accept you at once; if you aren't they won't bother you – but they won't think about you, either.'

'Well, that's all I want. I wish I had stringy hair and a flat nose and buck teeth!'

'You'd hate it if you did,' Sue pointed out.

'I think you're *nice*,' said Tabitha, who had been listening closely. 'And I'll never say you're pretty – even if you are.'

Sue and Cal both laughed, and Cal stood up. 'I guess I ought to go now,' she said. 'Cornelia told me not to stay long. It's been awfully nice. May I come again? I – I get sort of lonesome, at home.'

'Come any time,' said Sue warmly. 'And Cal – are you sure you wouldn't like to meet some of the boys and girls in the neighbourhood?'

'No, thank you. I'd rather not, if you don't mind.'

Sue went to the door with her, and watched the odd, lonely child turn homeward on slow feet.

5

Cornelia

THAT same evening after the children were in bed the Barrys and Veazie Ann were having after-dinner coffee in the living-room – a custom thoroughly enjoyed by Veazie Ann, who disapproved of it.

'The place for dinner,' she frequently remarked, leaning back comfortably, 'is on the dining-room table and have done with it, and not be a-finishing in shiftlessness in the front room, with a mess of dishes a-staring at ye.'

'They can't possibly see you from there,' Sue had once pointed out, 'but we can all go out in the kitchen and have our coffee over the sink, if it will make the dishes feel any better.'

'Likely 'twould, but I wun't. There's no call to let things like that git the better of ye. I had a ironstone platter one time, that did, and life warn't wuth living. Let 'em wait.'

Tonight, Sue and Veazie Ann occupied the long couch before the fire. Sue had changed to a soft blue housecoat which gave her skin a delicate freshness and brought out the copper lights in her hair. Her long flowing skirt spread out on either side of her, and beside Veazie Ann's serene bulk she looked like a slim blue moth.

Bill had pushed his armchair back from the fender and now sat staring into the fire. He looked tired, Sue thought; but she had never known a doctor who wasn't tired. It was a merciless profession, even with the supposedly regular hours of a hospital superintendent who had two interns attending to routine problems and detail. Well, it had been a pleasant, relaxing afternoon, except for Jerry's performance and tomorrow was Sunday. If there were no emergency calls from the hospital Bill could sleep late and have another leisurely day.

Sue watched him sympathetically from beneath her lashes, wondering what he was thinking. After all this time she still couldn't guess – at least, not very often. Bill had a quiet, penetrating mind, very different from her own quick practicality and acceptance of life from day to day.

A good marriage, Sue thought, got better as it went on. In the beginning she had supposed that it was entirely a matter of I-love-you-and-you-love-me. There was a lot more to it than that. The first two or three years were a strain; it was all too new and exciting, and you weren't used to one another. Then there was a slack pace when you didn't know quite where you were – but after that you began to settle in, and your marriage *really* became 'we' instead of 'I'.

Bill stirred in his chair and looked up. 'What,' he asked, 'possessed Jerry this afternoon? The children have been warned a dozen times about open windows.'

Sue didn't reply at once. 'I don't know,' she said at last. 'I think he just forgets. His mind seems to be somewhere else about two-thirds of the time.'

'That's right,' said Veazie Ann unexpectedly. 'Jerry don't always hear what's said to him.'

'Johnny and Tabs hear all right,' Bill said, 'unless they're pretending. But Jerry acts like somebody with a permanent hotfoot – completely absorbed with his own private irritation.'

'But why?' Sue asked. 'There must be some reason.'

'Well,' said Bill slowly, 'four and five are tough ages – a kid is passing from babyhood into childhood, and it takes some harder than others. If that's it, it'll wear off. If it isn't, the reason is bound to come out sooner or later.'

'That's great! When you find out you can let me know care of the Sanitorium for Mothers with Nervous Prostration.'

'I'll write you,' Bill promised, and added suddenly, 'By the way, who was that terrific youngster who was here this afternoon – Cal Somebody. I could swear I'd seen her somewhere.'

'She's our new neighbour in the Irwin place. Her mother is the artist.'

Bill sat up and so did Veazie Ann.

'Mona Stuart?' Bill exclaimed. 'I didn't know she had a kid. No wonder she looked familiar. She must have been Mona Stuart's model for the "Girl with Catkins".'

'She was, but for heaven's sake don't ever mention it to her. She's got a Thing about it.'

'Well I never!' said Veazie Ann. 'Everybody was talking about that woman at Ladies' Aid – especially Nettie Littlefield – but I don't believe there was a soul knew there was a young one. Seems odd, don't it?'

'Anything,' Bill drawled, 'that gets by Nettie Littlefield is darned odd.'

Veazie Ann chuckled. 'Nettie ain't curious – she just wants to know. Sometimes I think –'

'Well, I'm curious,' Sue interrupted. 'What did they say at Ladies' Aid?'

'Mostly that folks was funny, and if a body could get their own way as teetotal as that Stuart woman, they'd ought to be real pleasant.'

'Isn't she?'

'Not according to Nettie, she ain't. Seems as though bears would be a sight easier to have around.' Veazie Ann paused.

'Go *on*!' Sue wailed.

'All right. I'm a-telling ye. Seems Amos Littlefield done some of the carpentry and painting over to the Irwin place. Oliver Prouty hired him. Well, the Stuart woman, she come back and forth from Boston while the work was a-going on, and the fust time Amos see her he'd no idea who she was.'

'What does she look like? Somebody must have said.'

'Amos said. He says she's short and kind of dumpy, with black hair, worn in a bun on top of her head – the old-fashioned way. And she's got gimlet eyes, real black, that'd look right through ye and come out t'other side. Amos says he never see her without she had on one of them long white coats – same's Bill wears in the hospital. And paint spots on it.'

'Well, oil paints don't come out,' said Sue reasonably.

'I'm only telling ye what Nettie said Amos said. Anyhow, he kind of figured she was the housekeeper, fust off. Looked like her feet hurt her, he said. But then she come and stood over him.

'He swears up and down she barked like a fox. "Take that board off of there!" she says. "When I say nineteen and-a-half inches I *mean* nineteen-and-a-half inches! That's a quarter inch too narrow."

'Well, Amos, he figured there wasn't a woman living had that good a eye, but he's real mild-spoken, so he just kind of mumbled something about the owner.

' "I'm the owner," she says, "and you'll do as you're paid to do or get out." So Amos took the board off. But next time she come he was a-painting around them big windows she's put in, in the barn. She come a-stomping through the door, a-breathing, and she says, "Can't you put that on without slobbering it all over the panes?" Amos, he looked at her. "Nope," he says, "not without I make up my mind to."

' "Well, make your mind up then," she barks.

' "I have," says Amos, and with that he wrapped up his brushes and walked out.'

Sue was appalled. 'Goodness,' she said. 'Isn't she rather overdoing the arrogance?'

'Not necessarily,' Bill said. 'Remember, she's Mona Stuart. The woman's a genius, and I imagine she's been forced to build up that arrogance in self-defence.'

'What on earth do you mean? Who's after her?'

'Everybody, probably – so she's got to do what she can to keep her creative drive from being dissipated. The greater she is, the more the demands on her – but with a savage front like that she'll be let alone to work in peace. And she's right. She should.'

'But Bill – that unfortunate child!'

'I imagine,' said Bill, yawning gigantically, 'that she doesn't act like that with her child.' He pulled himself out of his chair. 'If you girls can stand the evening without me, I think I'll go to bed. Keep this weather another day, and I'll have the garden spaded and limed.'

'It'll hold,' said Veazie Ann, and she was right. When Sue went to bed, shortly before midnight, flat inky mountains were pasted against a spangled sky. Much later, waking automatically and going into the nursery to see if the boys had kicked off their covers, she heard the wind mumbling around the eaves, its winter whine gone. A lazy half-moon picked out only a few fat clouds strung along the hills. These crawled off as the sun rose, leaving dishevelled snow peaks behind them, and by the time the

Barry family was up and had eaten breakfast the sun was hot and the air was loud with the gorged pouring of brooks.

Bill and the children rushed out into the morning. Sue and Veazie Ann did the dishes.

'You coming to church this morning, Sue?'

'Not this time. I'd like to keep the children off Bill's neck, if necessary. Shall I drive you down?'

'Land, no! I'll stroll along and the Todds can pick me up when they come by. You take it easy this morning, Sue. There ain't much to do.'

There was upstairs work to be done, however, and after Veazie Ann had gone Sue paused for an automatic check-up on her family before she left them to their own devices.

Bill was staking out the vegetable garden at the foot of the hill pasture and the children were playing in the sand-pile. Their laughter sounded happy and sun-warmed, and they showed no inclination to interfere with the creation of the vegetable garden.

Sue went upstairs to make the beds, opening all the windows wide to let in the breath of the mountains and the thin, sweet sound of church bells ringing across the valley. One of the children – Jerry, Sue thought – began to sing with the bells. 'Bing-bong,' he chanted. 'Bing-bong.' He had chanced upon the exact pitch and his little voice became, suddenly, the heart of the spring morning.

Tabitha came up the stairs. Her nose was bright yellow from pollen and sand poured from her overalls in a gentle rain.

'Can I help, Mummy?'

'Of course, dear.'

Tabitha was a capable bedmaker and they worked together in pleasant silence; the child's face, between its dark, swinging plaits, was happy and intent. Sue smiled, watching her make a neat corner at the foot of Jerry's bed. She's *dear*, Sue thought. I'm *glad* I have a girl.

They finished the beds and tidied the bathroom.

'Are you going to do anything more, Mummy?'

'I'm going to take off these hot slacks and put on a nice cool skirt, and that's all until lunch-time. Scoot along and have fun – and thank you, darling.'

'You're quite welcome,' said Tabitha with an old-world courtesy that left her mother feeling slightly stunned.

Sue changed into a skirt and blouse, washed out a pair of Bill's socks and was hanging them on the line in the back yard when Johnny appeared in the barn doorway. He was carrying one of his usual, mysterious contraptions. He raced across the lawn, serious but eager. The sun made a halo of his tousled red hair, his blue eyes were almost violet with intensity, and he held out the contraption with both hands.

'Mummy! Mummy!' he yelled deafeningly from a distance of three feet. 'I made this for you; it's a beautiful doorstop for your room. You said you wished you had one.'

The doorstop was a cage made of lathes. It was rickety and uneven and bristled with nails guaranteed to catch anything and everything which passed it. It housed a morose and very muddy rock.

'Oh, Johnny! How wonderful!' Sue clasped it gingerly. 'It's just what I needed.' She bent to kiss the top of his head and found it exceedingly gritty.

Johnny gazed at her, crimson with gratification. 'I'll make you EVERYTHING, Mummy,' he shouted, and bounded away.

She looked after him in a sudden warmth of tenderness, wiped the sand off her mouth, and wondered what had come over her family. She stood for a moment clasping the doorstop. A soft breeze touched her cheek and the sun was warm on her shoulders. Sounds of hammering came from the barn, which meant that Johnny was happy. Tabitha and Jerry were engaged in a communal project involving their cart and a great many stones. They exuded harmony. The scrape of Bill's spade and the thump of turned clods added a final, peaceful touch to the morning.

Sue felt suddenly rebellious. There were still things to be done in the house – but she wasn't going to do them. She was going to do something that was fun – and silly – just for herself.

She considered and laughed aloud as she decided to give herself a facial. Her skin began, instantly, to feel dry, wrinkled, and hideously pitted with craterlike pores.

She turned briskly, went indoors and upstairs, placed the caged rock against her bedroom door, and hoped that it wouldn't tear Bill's flesh from his bones. Then, with the happy anticipation which every woman feels at the prospect of improving her appearance, she removed her blouse, retired to the bathroom, and was pinning a towel around her hair when Bill's voice rose from downstairs.

'Sue! Where the dickens is my box of socket wrenches?'

'Isn't it on the shelf in the back porch?'

'No, it isn't. I wish you'd keep Johnny out of my tools.'

'All right, dear. Wait a minute and I'll find it.' She put her blouse on and went to the rescue.

The box, however, was not in the house, nor in the barn. Sue found it at last under a burlap bag in the woodshed.

Bill looked sheepish. 'I remember now,' he said. 'I had it here yesterday.'

Sue nobly refrained from comment and Bill grinned. 'That's right,' he said. 'Nag! Nag! Nag!' He went away, pacified, and Sue went back upstairs, took off her blouse again, pinned the towel around her head, and another around her neck.

All her cosmetics were kept on the top shelf of the bathroom cabinet, well out of reach of her predatory sons. She was just about to take down a jar of cleansing cream when her hand paused in mid-air and her eyes lighted. There, still snug in its cellophane-covered box, was the far-too-expensive jar of facial clay which she had brought home from Boston and had promptly forgotten.

She took the box down and opened it. The jar wasn't very large, considering its price, but the clay was cool to the touch, delicately scented, and full of promise.

Sue applied hot towels to her face until it was a bright scarlet and she was just drying it when she heard somebody pounding on the front door. She called down the stairs. 'Hello?'

'It's me, Sue – Ira Prouty. Marianna sent you a present.'

'I'll be down in two seconds.'

Ira was the first real friend Sue had made when she came to Springdale as Public Health nurse. Furthermore, he had solved the problem of what to do with Marianna Lawson, the thorny and obstinate youngster whom Sue and Kit had brought with them from New York. She had run away from the nursing-school, she hated the country, she yearned to be a girl tramp, and was going from bad to worse when Ira, quietly but astoundingly, had married her. She had turned out to be an excellent wife, but she was still easy to offend.

Sue removed the towels, put on her blouse, and hurried down the stairs to receive the present in person.

It was a loaf of home-baked bread, for which Marianna was becoming locally famous.

'Oh, Ira! How gorgeous! How's the baby?'

'Cute's a bug's ear. Marianna says to ask you have you heard from Kit?'

'Not yet. I'll call her when I do. I wish Marianna would come over. That's the trouble with you people living way out of the valley. I never see you.'

'I know it – but now we've took to farming the place we don't never seem to git away from it. Well, I got to skedaddle.'

When he had gone Sue went back upstairs, established herself in the bathroom for the third time, and picked up the jar of facial clay. I'd better read the directions, she thought, instead of slapping the stuff on, any old way. For what it cost they ought to include a couple of Egyptian slaves to do it for me.

She sat down on the edge of the tub and read the instructions. They were on a very high plane.

'Ravissante's Scented Snow Clay,' she read. 'Removes the dingy veil which hides the real YOU. Smooth evenly on the face, allow to dry, then rinse off with clear, cool water. The younger, prettier person who will be revealed when the clay has done its splendid work – is the person you really ARE.'

'Heavens!' said Sue aloud. 'What am I waiting for?'

She spread the clay on her face with a liberal hand – there was just enough for one facial – and smoothed it to an even mask, contemplating her fantastic appearance in the mirror with satisfaction. She looked, she thought, like a gigantic and horrible insect, and she was just hoping that the children wouldn't see her – they'd be frightened to death – when the sharp, brassy clamour of the front-door knocker sounded through the house.

Sue gasped, her mouth an appalled red O in the lower section of the clay mask. Then she called out of the bathroom window, 'Who is it, please?'

'Is that Mrs Barry?' inquired an unfamiliar woman's voice.

'Yes, it is. Could I help you?'

'I'd like to speak to you for a moment about Cal – if it's convenient.'

Sue thought frantically, Cal's mother! I'd better see her. She called down, 'Certainly,' realized that she would need time to make herself presentable, and added, 'Please go right in and sit down. I'll be there in just a moment.'

She heard the front door open. Then, in bitterness of spirit, she doused the precious clay with cold water and watched it melt away, to flow briskly down the drain. Well, maybe it would do something for the pipes. She snatched off her towels, scrambled into her blouse again, seized a compact, and dashed downstairs, powdering her nose as she went.

But it was not Cal's mother in the living-room. The visitor was a stout, pleasant-faced coloured woman, hatless and dressed in a neat grey uniform. She rose as Sue came in.

'I'm Mrs Stuart's maid, Cornelia,' she said. 'I hope I didn't come at a bad time.'

'Not at all,' Sue lied. 'I'm delighted to meet you. Cal told me about you. Please sit down.'

Cornelia sat down with quiet dignity. 'I won't keep you long, Mrs Barry,' she said, 'but Cal don't talk about anything but the Barrys since she was over here. She don't make friends very easy, and I thought it best to speak to you about her. I worry about her.' She was taking in, as she spoke, not only Sue, but the entire living-room in a single appraising glance. It told Sue very clearly that Cornelia had also come to find out what kind of people the Barrys were.

This had Sue's hearty approval – but why wasn't Cal's mother doing it?

Cornelia answered the unspoken thought. 'I've had the raising of Cal since she was ten days old, Mrs Barry, and I was with her mother a long time before that. Mrs Stuart ain't like ordinary folks, you understand. When she's working she don't know about anything else – and she's mostly working – so I see to Cal.'

The children's voices shrilled suddenly in the kitchen. Three pairs of shoes clattered on the linoleum, crockery rattled, and the refrigerator door was opened and shut. Cornelia listened with a smile.

'I understand you have three,' she said.

'Yes. I know it sounds like a lot more, but actually that's all there are.'

'It sounds good, Mrs Barry. Our house is too quiet. I'd like to hear children's feet running around *my* kitchen.'

'You probably will. The children adore Cal, already.'

Cornelia's smile vanished. She looked down, played with a button on her dress, looked up, and said slowly, 'I'm afraid not, Mrs Barry. Mrs Stuart don't like anybody on the place, and children disturb her.'

'Well,' said Sue with a grin, listening to the clamour in the kitchen, 'I see what she means.'

Before Cornelia could reply the children, going back out-of-doors, slammed the porch door violently and there was an immediate response from the kitchen sink – a heavy muffled smash accompanied by thin tinkling, and what appeared to be a rifle shot.

'Ah,' said Sue philosophically, 'there goes the geranium, three glasses, and the dog's dish.'

Cornelia's face relaxed and her rich, warm laughter filled the room. 'It'll do Cal good,' she said, 'to be around somebody like you.' She sobered. 'I've done the best I could for her, Mrs Barry, but what I can do now ain't good enough.'

Sue nodded encouragingly and waited.

'The trouble is,' Cornelia went on, 'the child don't have the kind of life she ought. She's never had a home like this, with lots going on and nobody minding, and she's got some funny notions. I guess she told you. But when she come back from here she was all excited and chattering – the way she should be at her age. So I – don't like to bother you with it – but if she could come over – and if you could kinder talk her out of some of her ideas – I believe she'd heed what *you* say.'

'Of course! Let her come as often as she likes, and I'll be glad to do the best I can. I certainly agree with you about the notions – they're not good or normal. What does her mother think about them?'

'She don't realize how it is, at all, Mrs Barry. Cal don't go to her mother. The child loves her, but she don't have much to say to her.'

'That's too bad,' said Sue frankly.

'Yes'm, it is, but I don't want you to get Mrs Stuart wrong. She means good by Cal, but she don't understand what's important, and if she did she wouldn't know what to do.'

'Can't you tell her?'

Cornelia sighed. 'I did, M'am, but she just looks upset and says anybody as outside normal life as she is ain't fit to cope with a child. She says it would be worse'n the blind leading the blind – and I reckon she's right. She can't help it, Mrs Barry.'

'Would it do any good – after a while, I mean, when I've seen more of Cal – if I tried talking to her mother? After all, I'm a trained nurse, and it might –'

'Oh, no, M'am, Mrs Barry. Don't you! I wouldn't want

you to get into trouble.' Cornelia rose hurriedly. 'I'm obliged to you. I'll try not to let Cal be a nuisance.'

'Don't you worry about that for a moment.' Sue held out her hand and Cornelia clasped it warmly.

When she had gone, Sue went out to the kitchen to gather up the debris in the sink and repot the geranium. I'll bet I can straighten that kid out, she thought. But what a strange woman!

She was scooping up pottery, wet earth, and broken glass with a pancake turner when Tabitha opened the back door and halted, round-eyed.

'Mummy! Your ear!'

Sue put up her hand and a crumbling white clay cast of her ear dropped into it. Cornelia must have been startled, though she had not, by so much as a flicker of the eyes, betrayed the fact. Sue laughed.

'That, my darling,' she said, 'is something which, at great trouble and expense, has made my ear the younger and prettier thing it really IS.'

Tabitha giggled. 'Mummy, you're crazy!'

'Well – yes and no,' Sue told her. 'I prefer to think not, because I've got an extra job on my hands.'

6

The doctor's daughter

AFTER Cornelia's talk with Sue, Cal came over as often as she liked, and as soon as she was accustomed to the household's ways she was a great deal of help. She amused the children endlessly with stories and games; she wiped Veazie Ann's dishes; she washed the outraged Maxl; she helped Bill in the garden; she ran errands for Sue, and she thrived on all of it.

Most of all, however, she liked to be with Sue, listening to stories of hospital life and Henry Street. 'You know, Mrs Barry,' she said one day, 'it must be nice to have you for a mother. Lots of times when I'd think you'd be furious with your children you just get laughing. You act as if children were *fun*.'

Sue laughed. 'They are fun, Cal – though I have moments when I wonder if it wouldn't be simpler if I dropped them all down the well.'

Cal was serious. 'No, but really. I never knew anyone like you before. It isn't just with the children; you've had such a marvellous life, too.'

'I've had a very ordinary life,' said Sue, astonished. 'I can't imagine anything less spectacular than being a trained nurse, getting married, and having children.'

'Well,' Cal said wistfully, 'it's the sort of life I'd like to have. Would – would you teach me first aid and how to bandage? That is, if it isn't too much trouble.'

'Of course I will. It's something everybody ought to

know. Later on, if you like, I'll teach you something about home nursing.'

Sue began the lessons next day, and Cal worked hard, first because she wanted Sue's approval and later because she was really interested. Her enthusiasm was further increased by the fact that everybody in the neighbour-hood came to Sue with cuts, burns, sprains, and minor injuries in general. Whenever this happened Cal stood by, fascinated, handing Sue gauze, scissors, or antiseptic as required. In her interest she forgot to be self-conscious and Sue, noting this, was encouraged.

In the meantime, Sue had her own problems. As babies the twins had been healthy, happy, preoccupied with their feet, their bottles, and a repulsive pale-brown preparation labelled 'Liver Soup'. Later they were jointly interested in swings, tricycles, Babar the Elephant, and lamb chops. But now Jerry was becoming more and more of an enigma. He was moody as well as restless, which was something new, and one rainy day – the one which proved so disastrous for Tabitha – his behaviour was so strange that Sue was forced to admit that she didn't understand him at all.

The night before there had been a heavy rain and roar-ing wind and trees were down across the road to the village. Bill ploughed his way to the hospital on foot, and, since the school bus was not running, Tabitha remained at home.

Veazie Ann was awakened that morning with her shoulder and one arm stiff with rheumatism. Sue ordered her back to bed, turned the children loose in the attic to dress up, and then attacked the ironing.

Tabitha and Johnny appeared to be settled for the morning, but in less than twenty minutes Jerry was downstairs again. He played his record of 'Peter and the Wolf' seven times in succession, and finally wandered out to the kitchen, where he stared glumly at the raindrops trickling down the window-pane.

Sue looked up from her ironing to watch the dreary little figure. If only, she thought, he had some special interest, like Johnny. Feeling sorry for him, she asked, gently, 'What's the matter, Jerry? What are you thinking about?'

'The rain, Mummy.'

'Do you mean "the rain that's raining all around" or just the silver drops on the window?'

'I don't know.'

He was silent for several minutes. Then he turned suddenly. 'Does silver make a noise?'

Sue had been answering questions like this for several years and was only baffled for a moment. 'Yes, it does,' she said. 'I'll show you.'

She set her iron on end and went into the dining-room, where she opened a sideboard drawer. Jerry pattered after her, his eyes bright.

'Here,' she said. 'Listen!'

She picked up a silver fork and struck it on the edge of the sideboard. Then she held it to Jerry's ear. He listened intently to the low humming.

'Do it again, Mummy!'

Sue did it again.

'Let me! *Let me!* LET ME!'

He tried it, pleased. 'May I do a different one? Please, Mummy? Can I?'

It was Sue's wedding silver but she dismissed her qualms. 'All right, darling, but only the forks will do that – not the spoons or the knives. And don't hit hard.'

She left him there tapping and listening and returned

to her ironing, glad that he had at last found something to amuse him. She was hanging one of Tabitha's blouses on the back of a chair when he rushed into the kitchen waving a pickle fork dangerously near his eyes.

'Mummy! Mummy! This is the one!' He struck the fork on the sink and Sue bent over to listen to the thin sweet sound.

'It's nice, isn't it?' she said smiling.

But he had run to the window where, to her surprise, he did nothing for almost a minute. Then he tapped the fork on the sill and held it to his ear.

'Bing-bong!' he chanted. 'Bing-bong.'

'Oh,' said his mother, 'I see. It's the church bells.'

Jerry was outraged. 'No!' he cried. 'No, it *isn't*! *I'm* the church bells.'

'Well, all right, dear. Don't be cross about it.'

He looked vague and disappeared into the living-room where Sue heard him tapping intermittently. After a while the drumming of the rain stopped, and Sue looked hopefully at the sky. It would be nice if the children could go out, but there was no break in the clouds and a fine drizzle was still falling.

Sue gathered up an armful of clothes to be put away and went through the hall, carrying them carefully. She didn't see Jerry until she was half-way up the stairs. He was huddled on the top stair, clutching the pickle fork, and he looked at her with such wretched eyes that she was startled.

'Why, darling! What is it?'

He burst into tears. 'Mummy, I can't make it rain!'

Sue laid the clothes down on the stairs and put her arms around him. 'Darling,' she said, 'of course you can't. God makes it rain – not little boys.'

'But I *want* to make it rain,' Jerry wept. 'I want it

to be falling – and the rest, too. But there isn't *anything.*'

'I don't understand, dear. What is it you want?'

'I don't know.'

'Well, if you don't know, how can I help you?'

He stared at her, through tears. 'All right,' he said, at last. 'Never mind, Mummy.'

She kissed him and went on up with the clothes. When she returned he had moved, and she heard him wandering around the house, tapping and 'bing-bonging' drearily. Whatever he wanted she knew that it had been important to him, and that she had failed him. There had been a dismal, helpless withdrawal in that 'never mind', which had stabbed her.

It is alarming to realize you don't understand your own child, and Sue would have had a long talk about it with Bill, that night, if subsequent events hadn't driven everything else out of her mind.

Sue stacked the luncheon dishes, put the twins to bed for their naps, tried – and failed – to keep Veazie Ann in bed any longer, and was downstairs when the telephone rang.

It was a call from a woman who lived along the same ridge, but off the main road. She had learned that Sue was interested in antiques.

'I've got a rosewood bureau, hand painted, belonged to my great-great-grandmother,' she said. 'We got no use for it, it's too small, but I hate to see it going to any of them stramming city folks. It's been a-settin' in the attic, I dunno how long, but it's in good shape – if ye'd like to see it.'

'I certainly would!' Sue told her, delighted.

'Well, could ye come this afternoon? They tell me the road's clear, this end, and I'm going off tomorrow to visit my folks for a spell. I could do with the money.'

'Why, yes. I could come right away, in fact.'

It was an excellent time to go. Veazie Ann was up, the twins would sleep for an hour and a half, and Tabitha loved this kind of expedition. She was fascinated by houses, by furniture, and by grown-up conversation. Also the sun was beginning to break through the clouds. The afternoon would be lovely.

Sue changed and hurried the pleased Tabitha into a clean dress and her best coat. Then they went out, accompanied by Maxl, to remove the back seats from the station wagon – a procedure which annoyed Maxl to such an extent that he refused to go, and waddled indignantly back to the house, very long-eared.

'You know, Mummy,' Tabitha said, as the car emerged from the lane and turned up the highway, 'when Maxl gets mad, he's madder than most anybody. He's a terribly important dog.'

'I know. He won't speak to us when we get back.'

Sue glanced down at the earnest little figure beside her. What an endearing face the child had, with her transparent skin, her blue eyes and sweet mouth, and her funny little nose which was still indeterminate, but would some day be very straight.

She's got a sensitive face, Sue thought, but not a weak one – not with that chin. She's going to be all right.

'Mummy,' said Tabitha, 'this is nice, isn't it?' She gave Sue one of her sudden, radiant smiles of pure happiness.

'It's very nice, darling,' Sue said, engulfed by a wave of tenderness.

'What are we going to buy?'

'A bureau, I think – a very old one. We have to go up in a lady's attic to see it, first.'

Tabitha's eyes widened in delight. 'Oh!' she cried. 'Really in somebody's *attic*! How *wonderful*!'

That was another thing about Tabitha, Sue reflected. She had a capacity for enjoyment which was even greater than her capacity for grief – and that was considerable. Alone, with her like this, she was a delightful companion.

They talked together happily until they reached the turn-off, and then Sue's attention was wholly on the road. It was clear of fallen trees, as promised – apart from a single limb, a few yards from the highway. Sue stopped and tried to drag it to one side, but though it was only three or four inches thick it was very long and one end was half buried in an embankment. She was unable to move it and finally bounced cautiously over, while Tabitha shrieked with satisfaction.

Beyond, the road was stony and rutted and it was some time before Sue and Tabs reached the lone farmhouse and the pleasures of the old-fashioned attic with its festoons of dried apples, its kegs of multicoloured beans, and its dust-covered, ancient trunks. Tabitha was charmed with everything, and had no desire to go home when the taciturn farmer came to carry the bureau down and load it into the station wagon.

Tabitha climbed into the front seat and they drove away at last, both well pleased. The car was half-way to the main road when Tabitha asked if she might go around back and look at the bureau.

'It's sweet,' she begged, 'and I want to see the flowers painted on the drawers. Please let me!'

'All right – but be careful not to get bumped. This road is no joke.'

Tabitha squeezed around the seat, and Sue heard her chirping over the bureau. 'It's kind of little, Mummy, but it's so smooth. Just look! The drawer handles are *beautiful*!'

The drawer handles were of hand-hammered brass, set

into filigree plates, but Sue was in no position, at the moment, to look at anything but the road, and as they approached the fallen limb she said, over her shoulder, 'Sit down, Tabs – and hold on tight.'

All right,' said Tabitha, gleefully, after a minute. 'I'm sitting.'

Sue had meant that Tabitha was to sit on the floor of the car. It didn't occur to her that the child might pick the top of the bureau as a place to settle. The front wheels rolled up and across, not too uncomfortably, but the rear of the car, being springier, came down with a violent bump in spite of skilful driving.

There was a scrambling thud and a shriek, which changed to howls.

'Mummy!' Tabitha bellowed. 'I fell.'

Sue stopped the car and looked back. The middle drawer of the bureau was partly open, and Tabitha was struggling to her feet from the floor beside it.

'My leg!' she wailed. 'It hurts!'

She looked down and shrieked again, this time in terror.

'It's *bleeding*! Mummy! Mummy!'

It was indeed bleeding – pouring, in fact, down Tabitha's leg into a spreading pool on the car floor.

Tabitha's yells ceased from sheer paralysis of fright.

Sue never remembered getting over into the back of the station wagon, but by the time she reached Tabitha her professional mind had taken firm charge of her emotions.

A vein had been cut, she saw – not an artery, for the blood poured steadily in the split seconds before her hands closed around Tabitha's leg, below the jagged wound which was on the inner side, just under the knee.

The flow became a trickle, a slight ooze – stopped.

But she couldn't kneel here indefinitely, holding it back. She must contrive some kind of tourniquet and reassure the blue-faced Tabs who was looking at her mother in desperate appeal.

'Darling,' said Sue's professional voice, 'don't be frightened. I'll fix it. Does it hurt much now?'

'N – no. It – it's the blood, Mummy.'

'But blood isn't anything, my sweet. I've told you that. And anyway, it's stopped. Can you help me a little by doing what I tell you?'

'I'll try?' Tabs quavered.

'Good! Then sit down against the side of the car. That's a little hard when I'm holding your leg, but you can do it. That's right. Now take hold of your leg, just the way I'm doing – hard – with both hands.'

Tabs leaned against the car and gripped with both pudgy hands, just above Sue's.

'That's my girl! Squeeze! Squeeze harder! I'm going to find something to tie around so we won't have to hold it. Let's see how you're doing.'

Sue let go, and there was an instant welling of blood. Tabitha whimpered.

'Hold tighter,' Sue ordered. 'Terribly tight.'

The flow ceased and Tabitha looked up proudly, a little more colour in her face.

'Splendid,' said Sue. 'Even Cal couldn't do better. Hold it just like that, and if it starts to bleed *don't let go*! Grab harder!'

'All right, Mummy.'

Sue was thinking rapidly. There was no use in trying to tear a piece out of her dress or Tabitha's. The material was new and tough. She thought briefly of rubber-covered light or horn wires in the car. No, she'd be for ever getting them out. And she had brought no handkerchief. What was worse, her bag had no strap on it long enough to go round.

She glanced out of the car window, and brightened.

'I'll be right back,' she told Tabs, and jumping out of the car, leaped across the ditch and up the low embankment to the field beyond. She snatched a large handful of long grass, twisted it, and tried it on her own ankle. A few of the stems broke, but the general mass held firmly. Now for a stick!

She hurried back to the fallen limb and broke off a sizable green twig.

'Here we are,' she said to Tabitha. 'Hold on just a second more.'

She tied the twist of grass in place, thrust the stick through the knot and turned it.

'That *hurts*, Mummy,' Tabs protested.

'I know, dear, but we can't help it. It's just till we get home. You hold the stick so it won't turn back.' She lifted Tabs over into the front seat. 'Keep your leg straight out, darling. I'll get home as fast as I can, and we'll call Daddy.'

The car tilted on to the highway, and Sue stepped on the gas, one eye on Tabitha's leg. There would have to be stitches – and quite a disinfecting job, for a flap of skin was turned in. Furthermore she didn't know how long Tabitha would be able to keep the grass tourniquet tight. Poor baby! She was crying quietly, now, and Sue made no attempt to stop her. The child had had a shock and this was a good way of getting it out of her system.

'What cut you, Tabs? Do you know?'

Tabs shook her head. 'It was something on the drawer,' she said through tears. 'Mummy, my leg aches. This grass thing hurts. It's too tight.'

'I know, dear, but it'll have to stay. We'll be home in a

minute. After all, don't forget you're a doctor's daughter, so try to be brave.'

Tabitha's chin came up. Without a word she tightened the tourniquet, and sat holding it grimly.

The car flashed down the road, faster than Sue had ever driven it before. She hoped that she wouldn't get arrested for speeding – but just let somebody try to stop her!

No one tried to stop her. There wasn't a police car or motor-cycle on the road, and when she swung into her own lane the grass tourniquet was still holding. Sue knew it must be miserably painful for poor Tabs by this time, but the child made no complaint.

She carried her into the house, causing intense excitement in the twins who had just come downstairs, and who trailed after her into the living-room where she put Tabitha on the couch, indifferent to blood on the new slip cover. Veazie Ann, apart from a startled exclamation, asked no questions but brought Sue her Henry Street bag and stood by for further orders.

Sue's first impulse was to send the boys out, but their interest and awed excitement cheered Tabitha, and Sue let them stay while she put on a pressure bandage in place of the tourniquet.

Then she called Bill and told him what had happened.

'It's jagged and dirty,' she finished. 'About two inches long and clear to the bone, I should say.'

'Good Lord! The poor kid! And you can't bring her down here. The road is still blocked. But it sounds to me like a case for general anaesthesia.'

'I'm sure it is. It's going to be quite a job.'

'Then she'll have to have a straight ether induction, I'm afraid. I can't possibly get a gas-and-oxygen machine up there on foot, and I doubt if Novocain –'

'It's too long a job for Novocain, Bill. She couldn't possibly keep still. She's been swell, Bill – she helped and was so good. But I'll never go anywhere again as long as I live, without my Henry Street bag.'

'Don't blame you. Well, I'll be home as fast as I can.'

'All right, but don't bother bringing one of those infernal masks. I'll make a really *good* cone, right here at home. And hurry, Bill!'

'Okay, dear. Don't worry. And tell the baby I love her.'

Sue hung up and returned to Tabitha. 'Now look, sweet, we're going to have to do some special, careful things to that cut. We don't want it to hurt you, so when Daddy comes I'm going to give you something to smell that will make you go sound asleep. You won't like the smell but when you wake up your leg will be –'

To her surprise Tabitha had brightened perceptibly.

'Oh!' Tabitha said, enthusiastically. 'Am I going to have an anaesthetic? Like in Daddy's hospital?'

'Just like in hospital,' Sue answered, reflecting that being a doctor's child had certain advantages. 'And Daddy told me to tell you he loves you.'

'Well, I knew that,' Tabitha said, complacently.

'Oh, you did, did you?' Sue smiled at her, and ran upstairs for some of the cardboard which had come back in Bill's best shirts from the laundry. Then she dug out one of the twin's old diapers, some gauze, and a safety pin.

I believe, she thought, that I'll make this in front of Tabs, so she can watch and have it all explained. Then it will be familiar and she won't be frightened.

She carried the things downstairs and sat on the couch with Tabs, explaining as she worked, and wishing that

Bill would come. Tabs's bandage was beginning to stain – not alarmingly – but more than it should.

Sue rolled the cardboard into a cylinder which she flattened into an oval, and did some complicated folding of the diaper, through the inside and over the outside, where she rolled it tightly, as one rolls a stocking. Then she stuffed gauze into one end, pinning it through the cardboard. It was the old, familiar ether cone of her student operating-room days, and she had always preferred it to any other kind.

Tabitha and the twins were interested and full of questions. Only once was Tabs dubious, and that was when Sue asked if she'd like to try the cone over her face. 'No, I wouldn't,' Tabs said, hurriedly.

'Well, you don't have to, darling. I'm not going to hold it close to your face anyway. I'm going to hold it quite a way off – so you can talk to us, and look around.'

'What's the stuff that smells, Mummy?'

'It's called ether and it looks just like water.'

'Ether! But that's what you're always saying Daddy smells of. I don't think that's such a horrid smell. I've smelled it on Daddy ever since I was young.'

Sue managed to keep her face straight. 'Well, just the same,' she said, 'you may not like it at first – but you'll get used to it after a minute.'

'I don't think I'll mind, Mummy,' Tabitha said. 'But what is Daddy going to *do* to my leg?'

Sue hesitated. The idea of having one's own flesh sewn up is disconcerting to anybody, but Tabitha had never in her life been told anything but the truth by her parents, and there seemed no way out of this.

'Uh –'. Sue began, trying to be casual – 'I expect he'll have to fasten the cut together very carefully and –'

'Oh,' said Tabitha brightening. 'You mean he's going

to *suture* it. Will he use nylon? He said the other day it
was the –'

'He didn't say what he was going to use,' said the
staggered Sue, wondering what else Tabitha had picked
up from her parents' conversation, and feeling that, on
the whole, it would be more comfortable not to know.

'I'll just look out and see if Daddy's coming,' she said,
and went over to the front window. There was no sign
of Bill yet, and Sue turned to the twins, still hovering in
silent fascination over Tabitha's leg. 'Boys, I want you to
put on your things and go out-of-doors to play until I
call you. It's nice out – but have Veazie Ann put on your
wellingtons.'

'Why can't we stay?' Johnny demanded. 'I want to
help Daddy.'

'When you're older, darling. Just now it would help
more if you went out.' Sue's tone was uncompromising
and the twins obeyed without argument.

When they had gone she saw that the staining on
Tabitha's bandage had begun to spread. She renewed it,
more tightly, and had just finished when Bill came in
through the kitchen with his bag.

'We'll need you,' Sue heard him say to Veazie Ann.
'Will you clear the kitchen table and cover it with a sheet
over a blanket? And I'd like another, smaller table, close
by. After that, stick with Sue, will you? She'll tell you
what to do. Think you're going to mind this?'

'I dunno for sartin, Bill, but seems as though if you and
Sue can do it – when it's your own child – I'd oughter be
able.'

'We've had more practice,' Bill pointed out. 'Though
I can't say I'm looking forward to this job.'

He came in to Tabitha, then, and she held out her
arms to him.

'Oh, Daddy, I thought you'd never come! But I've been good, haven't I, Mummy?' She added in exact imitation of Sue's tone, 'After all, I'm a *doctor's* daughter.'

Bill blinked and looked down at the dark little head against his chest. 'That's right,' he said. 'But what has the doctor's daughter been doing – cutting herself all over the place?'

Tabitha giggled. 'It was only one place, Daddy.'

'Well, that's enough. I found out what cut you when I came by the station wagon.'

'Oh! What was it?'

'There was a bureau drawer half open, and a corner of one of the plates that holds the handles was bent out. It was pretty sharp. I'll fix it tomorrow – but right now I'm going to give you a shot – a little one.'

'Oh, dear!' Tabitha began. And then, stoutly, 'All right, Daddy.'

Afterwards, Sue followed Bill out to the kitchen, where he took a can of ether from his coat pocket.

'You start her,' he said, 'while I get my stuff laid out and scrub. But run her light, Sue.'

Sue punched two small holes, with a safety pin, in the soft sealed top of the ether can. 'I'll put her under on the couch,' she said. 'It'll be less frightening – don't you think?'

Bill nodded and Sue returned to the living-room, where she slid Tabitha down flat on the couch, talking to her cheerfully, meanwhile. Then, sitting down on the couch behind Tabitha's head, Sue spilled two or three drops of ether into the gauze of the cone, which she held at least a foot away from the child's face.

Tabitha sniffed uncertainly, but the cone was too far away for the ether to choke her, and after a moment she relaxed.

'Just breathe, my darling,' Sue encouraged her as Veazie Ann came quietly into the room and sat down, to enclose Tabitha's small hand in both of hers.

Sue added a few more drops of ether and, after a moment, moved the cone a little nearer to Tabitha's nose.

'How is it, dear?' Sue asked.

'It's *cold*,' said Tabitha in a surprised voice. 'But I don't mind *very* much.'

'That's the girl! Shut your eyes, now, and take some big breaths.'

Tabitha did so, and Sue increased the ether.

It was a slow process, for Sue was determined not to hurry the child, and it was several minutes before Tabitha looked up. 'I feel swimmy,' she said.

'That's fine,' Sue told her. 'You're doing beautifully, Tabs. Daddy will be proud of you. Why, you'll be asleep in another second.'

It was a little longer than that, but presently Sue laid a folded handkerchief over Tabitha's eyes to protect them from the ether fumes, and brought the cone down close.

Tabitha's breathing quickened slightly, but she didn't move.

In the stillness Sue could hear the water running in the kitchen sink, and the sound of scrubbing. She sat listening to Tabitha's breathing, adding ether little by little. At last she turned back a corner of the handkerchief, and raised one of Tabitha's eyelids.

It seemed strange and somehow shocking to look into the fixed blue eye of her child and note that the pupil was contracted. Still, it must be done. Sue glanced at Tabitha's chest, saw that her breathing was no longer shallow, but deep and quiet and coming from her diaphragm.

'She's ready,' Sue called to Bill.

'So am I.'

Veazie Ann, without being told, lifted the limp little body tenderly while Sue held the cone, and together they moved Tabs to the kitchen and put her down gently on the big table.

Bill was waiting, his coat off and his shirt sleeves rolled above his elbows. A small table beside him was covered with a sterile towel on which he had spread a handful of instruments, needles and sutures, antiseptic, sulfa powder, and gauze sponges.

He listened intently to Tabitha's breathing and then said to Veazie Ann, 'Will you cut the bandage off for me, please? No! *Not these scissors!* Use the kitchen scissors.'

Whatever Veazie Ann may have felt, she cut away the pressure bandage without hesitation, and if she caught her breath at the sudden welling of blood, no one noticed. Bill was clamping the cut vein and tying the severed ends, was cleaning the wound thoroughly, was putting in sulfa powder.

Outside, the twins shouted at their play, and Maxl scratched irritatingly at the back door.

At last Bill picked up a long-handled, snug-nosed instrument, fastened it to one of the needles, and began to draw together the deeper muscles in the wound. This done, he examined the irregularly cut skin, fitted it together neatly, and with painstaking care began to suture it.

Sue took off the ether cone – permanently.

There were twelve stitches, and by the time the last one was tied and Bill was reaching for a bandage Tabitha had begun to move.

Bill grinned and looked up at Sue. 'Nice work,' he said.

He carried Tabitha upstairs to bed, with Sue close behind, and they tucked the now-muttering Tabs in among the blankets.

'Well,' said Sue, 'she's been swell! She's the doctor's daughter all right, but frankly, the doctor's wife is going to sit down!'

Bill wiped his forehead with his bare forearm.

'So,' he said, 'is the doctor!'

7

Mrs Barry is most kind

'It's all wrong,' said Sue. She was standing at the back-kitchen window, her elbows on the sill and her chin resting on a damp dish towel which dangled from one hand.

Veazie Ann closed the oven door and straightened up. Then she crossed to the window to look out and her round face broadened with pleasure. 'Be you crazy?' she inquired.

The apple tree in the back yard was in full rose-white bloom and Cal was boosting the children up on the low flowering branches. All four were laughing and happy, entirely in harmony with the blossoming morning.

'What's worrying ye?' Veazie Ann persisted. 'They ain't a-going to fall, and 'twouldn't matter if they did – the ground's as soft as a sponge.'

'I don't mean the children. I mean Cal. Look at her! She's fourteen years old, and her only friends are grown people or children of four and six. She's improved in a lot of ways, but I can't budge her on that one.'

'Ye got to have patience, Sue. Girls that age git spells.'

'I know, but this is more than a spell. She'll never develop normally if she doesn't snap out of this and make friends among children her own age. And how's she going to do that if she won't?'

'I dunno. It's kind of a problem. Tommy Bingham delivers their milk and he told his mother Cal was real

pretty, but every time he spoke to her she stiffened up like
a pillar of salt. Said she made him feel about nine feet
high and a-spouting fire. It's too bad.'

'Yes, it is.'

'Have ye talked to Cal about it?'

'I haven't had a chance – unless I wanted to force the
issue. Cal avoids the subject like the plague.' Sue paused,
picked at a speck on the window sill, looked up, and said,
'Maybe that's it. Maybe I *ought* to force the issue.'

'What was you figuring on doing?'

'I hadn't figured, but I am now. I'm going to give Cal
a party, whether or no.'

Veazie Ann looked dubious. 'Ain't that kind of like
pushing her off'n the Grand Banks to learn her to swim?'

'No – because I'll be right there to pass her the water
wings. And it won't be the Grand Banks anyway; it's
going to be a very small party with the friendliest kids
I can find – and I'll tell them ahead of time that Cal is
shy.'

'But she ain't – she's just plain contrary.'

'There's more to it than that, but I can't explain it to
the kids, and they'll understand shyness and excuse anything she does on those grounds.'

'Cal ain't going to cotton to it.'

'I'll manage her,' said Sue confidently, and, as usual
when she had decided on a course of action, she wasted no
time, but dropped the dish towel on the kitchen table,
opened the door, and went out to the apple tree, where
she drew Cal aside. They sat down cross-legged on the
grass in the warm sunlight and Sue explained.

As Veazie Ann had predicted, Cal didn't take to the
idea.

Her high colour faded and her grey eyes darkened in
panic. 'It's awfully nice of you, Mrs Barry,' she faltered,

'but I –' The formula for courteous refusal failed her and she blurted out, 'Oh, *please* don't! I *loathe* parties! Please don't give one for me!'

'Have you been to any in the last year or two?'

'*Yes!*' said Cal passionately. 'Cornelia made me go to some at school last winter, and it was like an awful dream. The girls kept whispering and giggling at me – so when the boys asked me to dance I – I fell all over them – so they stopped asking me unless Miss Harriman made them – and I just *sat* – and my *dress* was all wrong!'

This tale of woe was familiar enough, and though Sue, as a child, had been comfortably popular, she had seen more than one of her friends going through ordeals like Cal's. But they had all survived and triumphed. Sue remembered one girl who had spent the evening weeping in a corner at an eighth-grade party, and who, five years later, was elected Queen of the Dartmouth Winter Carnival. There was one aspect of Cal's story, however, which Sue wanted to investigate.

'What was the matter with your dress?' she asked.

'The colour. *All* the other girls wore pink or blue or white, but Mother said why look like something off a candy box, and she went out herself – I don't know what struck her – and bought me something in a sickly green. I heard one of the girls say I looked as if I'd been dipped in spinach soup.'

Sue's exasperation with Mona Stuart was increasing by the minute. Of course, Cal would have been stunning in a soft chartreuse but even a genius might be expected to understand the importance of dressing-like-the-other-girls.

'All right,' Sue gave in. 'If you don't like dancing we won't have that kind of party. We'll have a picnic at the lake, and all you'll need to wear will be jeans and a shirt and sweater. None of the girls around here wear anything else.'

Cal was still unhappy. 'This is awfully nice of you,' she said miserably, 'and I love a picnic – but couldn't it be just you and the children?'

'No, Cal, it couldn't. You really *must* make an effort to get over feeling this way. You're going to miss a lot of fun if you haven't any friends your age. You don't really want to be stuffy, do you?'

'No,' sullenly.

'Well, you're going to meet all these boys and girls in school in the autumn, anyway, and it'll be easier if you already know them. I realize that you had a tough time at Fenchley, but it won't be like that, here.'

Cal hesitated, and Sue added quickly, 'Tabitha and the twins will come, too – they'll love it.'

'Well –'

'Splendid! That's the girl! I'll write your mother a note.'

'Whatever for?' Cal asked wearily. 'Mother isn't interested. I'll just tell Cornelia.'

'But Cal, I can't give a picnic especially for you and not say a word to your mother. Of course I'll write her. Let's make it the twenty-third, shall we? School will be over then.'

'Whatever you say.' Cal was without enthusiasm.

Sue returned to the house before Cal had time to change her mind, sat down at the secretary in her living-room, and with a sheet of notepaper before her, sat considering lines of tactful approach.

If Mrs Stuart chanced to be as sensitive as she was formidable she might resent having an outsider doing what she ought to be doing herself, so there must be no

implied criticism. One should be as impersonal as possible – practically non-existent.

> Dear Mrs Stuart: [Sue wrote]
>   There is to be a picnic for some of the neighbour-
> hood children on Thursday, the twenty-third. We do
> hope that Cal can come and make some new friends.
>   Sincerely,
>   Sue Barton Barry

Sue re-read the note and grinned. There were advantages in being a genuine small-town matron. You could
write a vapid, innocuous note – the kind that Mona
Stuart would expect of such a person – and put yourself
out of all danger of antagonizing her.

Her strategy worked, for the next day Cal returned with
a reply.

> Dear Mrs Barry:
>   You are most kind. Cal will be delighted.
>   M. S.

'You've no idea what an achievement *that* is,' Cal told
Sue. 'Mother never writes to anybody, and when your
note came she just said, "Tell her all right." And then
Cornelia brought her a pen and paper and said, "Miss
Mona, you-all use your manners and write that lady
back." Mother muttered like anything, but she did what
Cornelia said.'

Sue was pleased. All that remained now was to arrange
the picnic, invite the guests, and see that Cal had such a
good time that her unwholesome resentments would be
permanently destroyed.

The picnic was no problem. A combination of the lake,
pickles, hamburgers, pop, cake, and a beach fire had
never failed to entrance Springdale's younger set. The

selection of guests was more difficult, owing to the tempo-
rary presence in Springdale of Amalie Rand, niece of the
local bank president.

Amalie had been removed, much against her will, from
a New York finishing school, and had been sent to Springdale to live with her aunt and her uncle while her parents
went to Italy. In her dark, old-for-her-age fashion Amalie
was very pretty – and anything but shy. Also, since her
mother's ideas on the care and supervision of the young
had been, to say the least, sketchy, Amalie was able to
enthral her classmates with first-hand accounts of theatres,
shops, and even night clubs, whose names, in Springdale,
seemed to come direct from the Arabian Nights.

As one worried parent remarked, it might all be in very
bad taste from an adult point of view, but it was un-
deniably the stuff to give the freshman class at Springdale
High, and for the entire winter Amalie had been the
centre of attention.

But she's not coming to *my* picnic, Sue told herself.
She'd make mincemeat of Cal in three seconds. I'd better
have a talk with Dexter and Cherry.

Dexter and Cherry Bonney were the two oldest children in a family of six, living a short distance down the
mountain from Sue's house. Dexter was president of his
class, and Cherry, though not a leader like Amalie, was
very popular. Both children were warm, friendly, and
unaffected.

Sue went to see them the next afternoon, and as she
drove into the yard the empty garage told her that Mrs
Bonney was not at home. The uproar from the house,
however, indicated that most of the young Bonneys were
there.

Dexter opened the door, letting out a blast of music
from the radio and a general racket of young voices. He

was a pleasant-faced boy with fair hair and frank blue eyes, and he seemed incredibly tall when Sue remembered the little boy of two years ago, who had not whimpered when she splinted his broken arm.

'Gee! Mrs Barry!' He flattened his cowlick with a hasty hand and yelled over his shoulder, 'Hey! Kids! Pipe down, will you! Here's Mrs Barry! Gee! This is great! Come on in.'

The living-room was large, sunny, and cheerfully cluttered with boots, jackets, baseball mitts, a home movie projector, a pinball game, and a great many children, who were again told to pipe down – and this time did so, somebody hurriedly shutting off the radio.

Sue found Cherry sitting on the end of the living-room couch engaged in the complicated process of giving the baby its bottle with one hand and holding the telephone receiver to her ear with the other.

'Well, I don't care,' Cherry was saying. 'I'd like to go Friday night, but I know Tommy can't ask me, and I'd rather go on my hands and knees than be seen with that poisonous Reed character. Did you see him in algebra? He thinks he's so –' she broke off abruptly.

'Oh, hello, Mrs Barry! Emmy, I'll call you back. Mrs Barry's here – and anyway, I'd better bubble the baby. So long.' Expertly, she threw a towel over her shoulder, upended the baby, and began to pat it between the shoulders. Between pats she cleared a place for Sue on the couch. 'Please sit down, Mrs Barry,' she said warmly. 'It's awfully nice to see you. Mother's out, but she'll be back pretty soon.'

'That's all right,' said Sue, wedging herself in the cleared spot, between a pile of school books and a dilapidated portable typewriter. 'I really came to see you and Dexter. I want you to do me a favour.'

'You bet!' said Dexter.

'Anything at all,' Cherry said.

Sue explained her project.

'Gee, that would be great!' Dexter said with enthusiasm. 'Cal Stuart? That one, I want to know. I saw her having a soda in Prouty's and bro-ther! I was blind for three days!'

'I'd like to know her too,' Cherry said, wiping the baby's mouth and returning the bottle to it.' Who are you going to ask, Mrs Barry?'

'That's what I came to talk to you about. Cal is agonizingly shy and rather scared about the whole thing. We don't want anybody who'll intimidate her. Who do you suggest?'

'Well, you'll have to ask Tommy Bingham,' Dexter said with a leer at his sister. 'He's Cherry's H.D.'

'What's an H.D.?' Sue inquired as the suddenly flushed Cherry glared at Dexter.

'Heart's Delight,' Cherry said. 'And he *isn't*! But Winnie Carter is Deck's, so you'd better ask her.'

'Tommy and Winnie would be fine,' Sue agreed. 'What about one more boy?'

'Howard Phinney?' Cherry suggested.

'Him!' Dexter said in disgust. 'He's no use. He's caught in the snare of the Big City.'

'He means Amalie Rand,' Cherry explained. 'Deck doesn't like her.'

'I sure don't!' Dexter said flatly. 'She's just a silly dope of a kid trying to act sophisticated, only most of the crowd are too dumb to see it. Cherry and Winnie are the only girls in school who aren't breaking out in a rash trying to imitate her.'

Cherry laughed and bubbled the baby again. 'I'd be a sensation, wouldn't I?' she said. 'Especially in that black jersey number she wore at the square dance at school.'

Cherry, Sue perceived, had enough sense to keep to a style that suited her. She might be too rosy and plump for the cover of a junior fashion magazine, but she looked exactly right in the full skirts and puffed-sleeved blouses that she wore.

'Howard's perfectly all right,' Cherry went on. 'I don't think he's any crazier about Amalie than the rest of the boys, and he's lots of fun. Cal might like him, once she got over the shock.'

Sue laughed, understanding the reference, for Howard, though barely past fourteen, was six feet tall, with wavy dark hair and liquid brown eyes.

'All right, then,' said Sue. 'We'll have Howard, and that'll make six, which is a good number – and enough for the first time.'

They were all such nice youngsters, too, she thought – all of them sensible, well-mannered, and sincerely friendly. Cal could hardly fail to get on with them, and if she became good friends with Cherry, who was a near neighbour, she'd not only have fun but the wholesome, lively Bonney household would do her the world of good.

And so, she told herself later, driving home, if the weather is good I won't have to worry about a thing.

8

The picnic

Bill,' Sue coaxed, 'look out and see if it's a nice day.'

'Huh?' said Bill drowsily.

'I said, look out and see if it's a nice day.'

Sodden with sleep Bill struggled up on one elbow and squinted at the windows. 'It's okay, I guess – hey! what is this? What's the matter with your looking for yourself?'

Sue was lying on her back with her eyes tight shut.

'I didn't want to be confronted by rain without knowing about it first. I wanted a chance to prepare myself.'

Bill lay down again. 'You ought to get out and meet some grown-ups. You spend so much time with the kids you're retrogressing right back into infancy. People will notice. Anyway, you can open up now. The sun *is* shining.'

She opened her eyes and sat up. Reflected golden light filled the room, pouring down from a clear blue sky. The leaves of the maypole hung motionless and across the valley among the tiered ranges there was no cloud to trace its pattern on the sunlit slopes.

'It's just right,' she said. 'I'll have no trouble at all.'

Bill gave her an odd, sharp look. 'I hope not, and I *hope* your plan works. I like that kid.'

'Well, you needn't sound so dubious. What do you mean by –'

She was prevented from further questioning by the arrival of all three children, none of whom was beset by

91

any doubts whatever. The twins climbed up on Bill's bed and flung themselves on him. Tabitha curled up beside her mother.

'It's a *beautiful* day,' Tabitha said. 'And Veazie Ann thinks it's going to be *hot*! Oh, Mummy, I'm so excited! Do you think Cal's excited too?'

'I expect so.' Sue waited for Bill to comment but he was busy disentangling himself from the twins.

There was no chance, later, to ask him what he had meant, for Sue was busy with the children and he had an appointment at the hospital immediately after breakfast, but Sue wondered uneasily what he'd been thinking. Why did he have to be so vague? It was irritating enough to have cold water thrown on your plans, without the thrower going off without explaining.

If he's had a better idea all this time, Sue thought, why didn't he say so?

Well, it was too late now. She turned her attention to the picnic, and immediately vital matters such as sandwiches, apple turnovers, grills, hamburgers, sarsaparilla, and dill pickles left her very little time to brood about Bill's unexpressed point of view. She was surprised when Cal presented herself at the back door.

'Goodness!' said Sue. 'Is it that late?'

'I'm early. Am I – is this what the other girls will wear?'

She was dressed in ordinary jeans, a boy's white shirt, and a leather belt. The only distinguishing note in her costume was the scarf she wore around her head – a soft scarf, oddly and delightfully patterned in tiny stripes – emerald, scarlet, deep purple, blue, and gold. It was scattered over irregularly with very small silver bells.

'You look lovely,' Sue assured her, 'and I like your scarf.'

'Is it all right?' Cal asked anxiously. 'Somebody in

New York gave it to me. I like it a lot, but I was afraid it might look – you know – funny.'

She was obviously thinking of the chartreuse dress and Sue hastened to reassure her.

'It's perfect,' she said. 'Come on – want to help load the things?'

'Oh – oh, yes! Certainly.'

'We're going to cook hamburgers *outdoors*!' Jerry cried,

'And we've got apple turnovers!' Tabitha supplemented.

The children's excitement communicated itself to Cal and for a time, while they were packing the station wagon, she seemed almost gay. Then Johnny glanced down the road and began to jump.

'Here come Winnie and Tommy and Howard!' he shouted.

Cal was suddenly motionless, her face as blank as a slammed door. She glanced at Sue only once, a strange glance, half resentful and half pleading. Then her face closed again.

Winnie Carter, flanked by the gangling figures of Tommy Bingham and Howard Phinney, looked very pretty, very tiny, and so incompetent that there hovered over her, despite her practical shirt and jeans, a distinct suggestion of organdie and ruffles. She was small and delicately bloomed, with the fluffy hair, short nose, and wide blue eyes of a Persian kitten. Actually, as all her friends knew, she was a hard-headed sensible girl who got straight A's in algebra and sold eggs at a profit.

She shook hands briskly with Cal.

'I'm awfully glad you're going to live here,' she said cordially. 'I hope you'll like Springdale High. We're getting a new cafeteria this year, and maybe the food will be fit to eat.'

'How do you do,' said Cal.

Howard Phinney stepped forward eagerly. 'I'm Howard Phinney,' he said, 'and I guess you know Tommy Bingham. Anyway, he claims you do.'

There was nothing deceptive about the appearance of either Howard or Tommy. They looked exactly what they were, tall, brown farmer's sons with the relaxed competence of boys who have spent their lives among crops and farm animals. But they had never before seen a girl as pretty as Cal, and though they didn't say 'Wow!' or whistle, they did stare.

'How do you do,' said Cal.

After that everybody was silent.

Fortunately, the Bonneys arrived just then, and more introductions were in order. Dexter was smiling and good-natured as usual. Cherry, her head covered with a red bandanna, and her pigtails festively adorned with scarlet ribbon, was sunnily pleasant.

'It's awfully nice to meet you at last,' Cherry said, smiling at Cal. 'We've heard lots about you. Mrs Barry says she's been teaching you first aid.'

'Yes, she has, thank you,' Cal said, so stiffly that a less amiable or well-bred girl would have ignored her from that moment. The kind-hearted Cherry paid no attention. Mrs Barry had said that Cal was shy, and that was enough for Cherry.

'First aid must be fun!' she said. 'Mrs Barry was wonderful when Deck broke his arm, and when Cathy – that's my baby sister – came home from the hospital, Mother said that after six she was a little overtrained on babies. She said the novelty had worn off, and I'd better start learning right away from Mrs Barry, so I could take care of the baby. It's a good thing I did, too, because Mother's really terribly old-fashioned.'

To Sue's relief, Cal, this time, displayed animation.

'Oh!' she exclaimed. 'It must be wonderful to take care of a baby! I'd love that! Do you give her her bath and everything?'

'Oh, yes,' said the proud Cherry. 'It's really very easy. Why don't you come over some afternoon at her bath time and I'll show you.'

'I'd adore to,' Cal said.

On this promising note Sue felt that they could safely start off for the lake. It seemed to her that her plan was already a success, and that by the end of the afternoon Cal would have plenty of friends her own age and would be no problem at all.

As she started the car down the steep winding road she thought comfortably that it was fun to be going on a picnic with a carload of chattering youngsters, fun to have Tabitha and the twins along and accepted.

She could hear Tabitha telling Dexter Bonney about the newt they had found and brought home.

'We keep it in a coffee pan with lots of moss and leaves and things,' Tabitha explained. 'And its name is Heidi.'

'Why Heidi?' asked Dexter solemnly.

'Because it hides, of course,' Johnny said, and Dexter agreed that, under those circumstances, Heidi was the only possible name.

Cherry and Winnie were discussing the French teacher who was in Cherry's opinion, more than somewhat super.

'You ought to speak French, then,' Howard said. 'You ought to say he's *très très* something or other.'

'*Joli*,' said Winnie, 'only I don't know if men are *joli*, but whatever it is, he's IT.'

'Cherry's stuck on him,' said Tommy sourly. 'But he's *très*, *très* something or other – giving me a C minus!'

'He's nice,' Cherry said indignantly. 'He was born in

Keene. I heard him telling Miss Elder about it, once.'

'Well, anyway, it won't help you to be stuck on him,' Winnie said. 'Elder's got her hooks in him. You'll have to make out with present company.'

'Perish the thought,' said Cherry.

The boys hooted, and Sue hoped that they would change to a more general topic. She was afraid that Cal would feel left out. On a level stretch of road, however, when she glanced in the rear-view mirror, she saw that Cal was not only listening attentively, but was smiling a little, and when the first blue line of the lake appeared in the distance Cal leaned forward with as much excitement as the others.

The lake sprawled along the valley, delicately blue, and spangled by the sun. Because it was shallow and fed by winding streams, it was paler than the deep-blue spring-fed lakes, and its clear waters warmed earlier in the season. On a little cove edged with fragrant spruce was a log cabin which served as a hunting camp in the autumn and a bathing-hut in the summer.

Cal sprang out of the car and helped Tabitha down.

'Do you like it?' Tabitha demanded with pride. '*We* think it's nice.'

'Oh, it's beautiful!' Cal exclaimed. 'It's *lovely*!'

'I hope,' said Winnie, 'that the water's warm enough. Howard and Deck were over here swimming last week and they said it was okay, but they'd think it was warm if it had cakes of ice floating in it.'

'It's lovely,' Cal said again. 'And so clear. Like water in a swimming-pool.'

She was animated and seemed entirely at ease, helping the others unload the station wagon and arrange the assorted packages on a flat rock beside the smoke-blackened outdoor fireplace. When the girls retired to the cabin to put on bathing suits Cal went with them, and though she wasn't chattering, she was at least talking without stiffness.

Sue was delighted. Why, she wondered, hadn't she had the sense to do this earlier? A good push was all, that Cal had needed. As for Bill and his dubiousness – for once he was wrong.

While the girls were undressing – the boys had worn trunks under their clothes – Sue got Tabitha and the twins into their own ridiculously small bathing suits and sent them scampering down to the sandy beach.

Cal and Cherry emerged together. Cherry was wearing a chintz two-piece suit patterned with strawberries and ruffled in red. She looked gay and pretty, but Cal completely eclipsed her in a plain green suit with the insignia of a girls' camp embroidered on it.

Howard and Tommy were too fond of Cherry to remark on this, but brothers have no reticences.

'My sister,' Dexter said, 'has a new bathing suit and thinks she's Something, but *you*, Mademoiselle –' he bowed elaborately to Cal – '*you*, Mademoiselle, are – are –'

'Belle,' the generous Cherry supplied. 'Mademoiselle *is* very *belle*.'

They all perceived the rhyme and began to chant it gaily.

'Mademois*elle* is awfully *belle*. Mademois*elle* is awfully *belle*. Mademois*elle* –'

They had no thought of teasing but were merely amused by their own nonsense, and were treating Cal as one of themselves. If anyone had the slightest reason for being annoyed it was Cherry, who, despite her new bathing suit, was not being called *belle*, but Cherry was laughing. It was Cal who was becoming stiff and white, Cal alone who didn't join in the laughter.

Sue's heart sank, and she longed to shake Cal.

'Mummy,' Tabitha demanded, 'what's bell? What kind of a bell?'

'It's a French word, Tabs, and it means pretty.'

'Well, she is,' said Jerry, taking Cal's hand.

Cal disengaged it gently, and, looking at nobody, said, 'Let's go swimming.'

There was a diving float in the centre of the cove and everybody plunged towards it except Sue, and, of course, the children. But when Cal was half-way out she turned and swam back.

'Wouldn't you like to swim, Mrs Barry?' she asked with deadly courtesy. 'I'll watch the children.'

'Cal,' said Sue, ignoring the offer, 'those kids didn't mean anything at all, and it's silly of you to think they did. It was a joke – and a compliment.'

Cal said nothing, but stood, waist deep in the water, her eyes on the distant mountains.

'I understand how you felt,' said Sue, 'but they didn't. How do you expect them to find out that you're a nice person if you never give them a chance?'

'All right,' Cal said. 'I'll try. But let me stay with the children for a while, first, and you go in. The water's wonderful.'

Sue hesitated and then agreed. It might be just as well if Cal did have a little time to herself. Sue was, in fact, grateful for a chance to swim. The mother of small children has few opportunities to practise her eight-beat crawl; she is too busy keeping her young from the watery grave into which they hurl themselves at sixty-second intervals.

She was almost surprised to find that she was still a good swimmer. This is a disgrace, she told herself, back-stroking idly as she watched the summer clouds tower overhead. I ought to be in uniform, making rounds, instead of picnicking irresponsibly with adolescents. What's more, I've even turned the children over to somebody else so I can admire myself as a swimmer!

Sue enjoyed her swim. The water was cool and tingling, but it had lost the paralysing cold of early spring and she went far out, returning flushed and stimulated. Cal was still in the shallows with the children but she had been joined by Howard Phinney, and to Sue's surprise she found that they were companionably engaged in teaching the twins to swim, and in instructing Tabitha in the mysteries of the flutter kick.

'This is swell of you,' said Sue peeling off her bathing cap and ruffling her flattened hair until it gleamed again, copper-red in the sunlight. 'Goodness! You've actually got Tabs so that she keeps her knees stiff.'

'Howard doesn't like to dive,' Cal said. 'He thinks it's more fun teaching kids not to drown than to be half-drowned himself.' She was obviously pleased with herself, for she had not snubbed Howard when he joined her. The presence of the children had helped, but Cal was really trying.

'I hate to break up the lesson,' Sue told them, 'but the children are beginning to look a bit blue. Anyway, isn't it time to eat?'

'It sure is,' said Howard. 'But don't you bother, Mrs Barry. Cal and I will fix everything.'

'Oh!' Cal said. 'Oh – I –'

'That'll be splendid,' said Sue as gratefully as though she hadn't heard the uncertainty in Cal's voice.

Cal splashed obediently out of the water and the others, on the float, seeing the stir of preparation, came hurriedly ashore. By the time Sue had the children dressed, the baskets and packages were open, the hamburgers were grilling over the stone fireplace, and Dexter and Tommy were gathering more wood.

No one had bothered to dress, and Winnie, in a practical, terry-cloth beach robe, was buttering hamburger rolls while Cherry searched for the bottle opener.

Cal had pulled a sweat shirt over her bathing suit and her hair fell damply about her shoulders, but she was rosy and cheerful as she helped Howard with the hamburgers and doled out sandwiches to the ravenous children.

It was obvious that Howard was dazzled by Cal almost to the point of speechlessness, but, being a level-headed boy, he merely gave her instructions and an occasional smile.

'This one's done – it's about right for Tabitha. Just hand me the buns, will you?'

Cal did as she was told. Later she ate heartily and though she only listened to the conversation she seemed to be having a good time. Certainly, she had no cause for complaint. Winnie and Cherry didn't whisper behind her back, and neither the admiration of Tommy and Dexter, nor even that of the smitten Howard manifested itself in any way that she could resent.

After lunch Dexter produced a medicine ball which everybody hurled about strenuously. Cal included, and Sue was congratulating herself again when, literally, in a cloud of dust and a thunder of hoof-beats, Amalie Rand appeared.

'Hel*lo* there!' she cried, pulling up. 'What goes on? A picnic! How nice!'

'Hello, Amalie,' said Sue, feeling murderous. 'How are you?'

'Perishing from thirst and exhaustion! And Centaur is all overheated. *Could* we stop here, and maybe cadge a "Coke"?'

'Of course,' said the trapped Sue.

Amalie swung expertly out of the saddle and tied her horse to the nearest stump. There had been a crisp precision in her horsemanship which was as different from that of the local children – accustomed to riding bareback on farm horses – as her beautifully cut jodhpurs and silk shirt were from the baggy jeans. Amalie's differentness in appearance, however, was solidly reinforced by a dominating personality.

Howard, who had been playing tag with Cal and the twins, hurried to bring Amalie a bottle of Coca-Cola. She gave him a grateful but competent stare, said that he had saved her life, and then, ensconcing herself in the centre of the group, took charge of the conversation, which she directed at Cal.

'You're Caroline Stuart, aren't you?' she began. 'I heard you went to Fenchley. Did you know Lisa Willard and Cass Lattimore?'

'They were in my class,' Cal said.

'They told me a lot about you. They were frightfully impressed at having Mona Stuart's daughter in school with them.'

Cal said nothing and Amalie chattered on.

'We studied your mother's work in art class, you know. I remember you in that picture.'

'Why Cal!' said Cherry, openly thrilled. 'Did your mother paint you? What fun! What was it like?'

By the set of Cal's mouth it was evident that she was not going to reply and Sue was actually grateful when Amalie answered for her.

'It's a wonderful picture – "Girl with Catkins", it's called. Lisa and Cass said you were much prettier in real life, and you are, only you seem small after the way I'd been thinking of you.' Amalie laughed. 'It is odd, you know, to meet somebody after you've seen them first on a six-foot lantern slide.'

Everybody turned to stare at Cal as if she had suddenly grown an additional head, and Sue tried to think of some way to end the conversation without resorting to such crude measures as hurling Amalie into the lake.

'Gosh!' Howard said. 'A real model in our midst!' The admiration in his voice was unmistakable and Amalie looked at Cal with sudden hostility.

'Oh,' she said sweetly, 'being a model is all right – I guess – if you *like* showing off. You must *adore* New York.'

'I *hate* New York!' Cal burst out.

'Well,' Amalie smiled kindly, 'perhaps you don't know the right people. I suppose your mother, being an artist, has some – odd – friends.'

Dexter Bonney, not ordinarily a sensitive boy, but a kind one, stood up suddenly. 'We're getting some darned funny people in Springdale, these days, too,' he said pointedly.

'Yes,' Amalie said, glancing at Cal, 'aren't we!'

Cal sprang to her feet, her face dead white.

'Can we play tag some more, Cal?' Johnny asked.

'Yes!' Cal said. 'Come on.'

She spoke to no one but the children for the rest of the afternoon. Once Sue approached her, but seeing that Cal was on the verge of tears, withdrew. It would be better to let her alone for now, Sue thought, but even after Amalie, well pleased with herself, had cantered away, Cal was unable to break her choked silence. She helped reload the station wagon, but she didn't change from her bathing suit to her clothes until Winnie and Cherry had left the cabin. On the ride home she said nothing at all.

Sue delivered the Bonneys at their door and Cherry, distressed and sympathetic, repeated her invitation to Cal.

'Please come over sometime when I'm bathing the baby,' she urged.

Cal managed to nod. 'Sometime,' she said, and there was flat refusal in her tone.

This time even the kindly Cherry lost patience. 'All right,' she said tartly. 'And Mrs Barry, thank you so much. We had a *lovely* time.'

'It was swell,' said Dexter. 'Good-bye, Cal.'

'Good-bye.'

Sue refrained from comment with difficulty, but when the last guest had been deposited she saw that the girl was openly in tears.

'Cal,' said Sue quietly.

'I know. I was awful. I did everything wrong. But I couldn't help it – it's always like that. Nobody ever sees anything but my face. Don't you understand?'

'I understand that everything was all right until that wretched Amalie Rand turned up. She was extremely rude, and you had every right to be upset – but it wasn't the others' fault. And it could have happened to anyone – Winnie or Cherry.'

'No, it couldn't, Mrs Barry. She acted like that because of the way I look. If it hadn't been her something else would have happened. It always does. *Always.*'

'Nonsense!' said Sue, and would have said more, but they had reached Cal's house now, and Sue was aware of her own children, worn out from sun, water, and excitement, drooping in the back of the station wagon.

As Cal got out she said hesitantly, 'Mrs Barry, are you – may I still come over to your house?'

'Of course you may, Cal.'

'Thank you – and I'm so sorry.'

When Sue got home she turned the children over to Veazie Ann and sank exhaustedly into a chair in the living-room.

Bill was lying on the couch, smoking and reading the afternoon papers. 'How did it go?' he asked.

'It was awful! Foul.' She told him what had happened and he nodded.

'I thought she'd clam up,' he said.

'Oh, for heaven's sake, Bill Barry!' said the tired and exasperated Sue. 'Why didn't you say so in the very beginning?'

Bill shrugged. 'I could have been wrong. After all, you know the kid better than I do.'

'But *why* did you think so? You've turned out to be perfectly right, so you can just put down that paper and explain.'

'Well,' Bill said, 'it seemed to me that you were working on the symptoms instead of the cause. It's perfectly clear that Cal believes her mother's only interest in her has been as a model – so Cal blames her looks for it. And she's gone right on from there, spreading it all over everybody, especially youngsters her age – who haven't much restraint and naturally do the most talking about it – just as they did today.'

'But –'

'Sue dear, the child is always going to feel resentful and insecure whenever her appearance is mentioned. There's no use trying to reason her out of it.'

'Then what would you suggest?'

'Get her together with her mother – if you can. Once Cal feels love and acceptance there, all this stuff about her looks and no friends will disappear so fast it'll make you jump.'

'But how in heaven's name,' said Sue, appalled, 'am

I to do that? I've never even spoken to the woman.'

Bill grinned. 'I'm the theorist around here; you're the gal who gets things done. How should I know how to patch up Cal and her mother? That's your department.'

9

Other people's business

TABITHA didn't want her breakfast.

It was not just an ordinary, don't-feel-like-eating occasion. That could have been ignored, for children's appetites are variable and Sue had never seen a child starve to death through missing an occasional meal. But Tabitha's attitude was by no means passive. She was miserable and determined, and from her point of view the sunny dining-room, the crisp tablecloth, the gay dishes, and her entire family, seemed enveloped in a thick, grey fog of gloom. Her mother's sympathetic face and the twins' cheerful appetites had no more effect than her father's quiet, 'Eat your cereal, Tabs.'

'Please, Daddy,' Tabitha quavered, 'I don't want my cereal. I *hate* oatmeal.'

'All right,' Sue agreed, 'would you like an egg?'

'No, thank you, I don't want an egg. I hate milk. I don't want any orange juice.'

'Tabitha,' Bill said, 'if you don't want any breakfast, how about going up to your room for a while, until you feel better?'

'I don't want to. I want –'

'All right, Tabs,' said Sue, 'that's enough. Either eat your breakfast or be quiet.'

Tabitha was quiet for the rest of the meal, but she could hardly be described as an asset to the jolly family group. She sat huddled in her chair, her lower lip quivering: she stared at the toaster.

'Wow!' Bill said to Sue, as he was leaving. 'I wouldn't be you! This is going to be one of Those Days.'

'It's a man's world,' Sue agreed. 'Here you are going off to your nice peaceful hospital, leaving me all alone with Tabs. I hope some good is going to come of all this temperament.'

She added, as she held up her face, 'I bet you were an awful little boy. She never got this from my side of the family.'

Bill grinned. 'A likely story,' he said, and kissed her.

When Sue went back into the house, the twins were already engaged in building a play pen for a moth-eaten toy seal, known, with an austere disregard for fancy names, as 'Sealy'. Tabitha was sitting in a heap on the back-porch steps.

'Why don't you go out and swing?' Sue inquired from the doorway.

'I don't want to swing.'

'Would you like to feed Maxl?'

'No, thank you,' said Tabitha, far from alight with a child's reputed affinity for dumb animals.

'Veazie Ann is making pies. Would you like to help?'

'No, thank you.'

'Well, then, what *would* you like to do?'

'I guess,' Tabitha said, brightening, 'that I'd like to wash all my clothes in the BIG washing-machine.'

'Oh, Tabitha,' Sue cried in dismay. 'Darling – you can't!'

'*Why* can't I?'

'Because you might hurt yourself. Even grown-ups have been hurt by washing machines when they didn't know exactly how to use them.'

Tabitha burst into tears.

'Oh dear!' she sobbed. 'Oh dear! Oh dear! I can't ever *do* anything! I can't ever *have* anything! I'm going away and *never* come back!'

She flung through the door and stumbled up the stairs to her room.

'Poor baby,' Sue said to Veazie Ann. 'She takes everything so desperately hard. I wish I knew what ails her this time. If it were winter I'd think it was something wrong at school, or that she was overtired – but this is vacation.'

'Likely that's the trouble,' Veazie Ann said. 'The child's bored. I can remember having spells like that when I was a young one. Seemed as though the minute I could play all I wanted to, I didn't know what to do. And 'tain't as if she could read good enough to keep herself amused.'

'I'll bet that's it!' Sue exclaimed, relieved. 'Well, I'll leave her by herself for a little, until she's calmed down, and then I'll see if I can think of something nice to do. We might go over to Echo Lake,'or Lost River. Of course I *was* planning to scrape the paper off the spare room today, but I suppose it'll keep.'

'You're a good mother, Sue. There's plenty wouldn't be bothered with a six-year-old's spells.'

Sue laughed. 'For heaven's sake,' she said. 'The child may be wretched about nothing, but she *is* wretched. I'm not going to fiddle with wallpaper when one of my children is unhappy – I don't care what it's about, or how silly it is.'

'That's what I –' Veazie Ann was beginning, when she broke off to stare out of the back window.

'Well,' she said, 'looks like Tabs has kind of taken things in her own hands.'

Sue turned quickly and saw, trudging along the path at the foot of the hill pasture, Tabitha's small, blue-overalled figure. She was hurrying, and the plaits behind her ears wagged in indignation.

Sue watched, longing to protect her child from even this small distress. 'The little monkey,' she said only half laughing, 'she really is leaving – and in high dudgeon, too.'

'Seems as though – but she's an independent little thing. Best leave her to work this out for herself.'

'Yes – but I think I'll just drift along behind and make sure that nothing happens to her.'

'Might as well. She's no need to know you're there.'

She waited a few minutes and then set out. Tabitha was half-way across the sunny meadow, the picture of out-raged childhood, determined to carve her own way in the world. So far she had not even paused to gather flowers or catch grasshoppers, but as the first driving force of her indignation lessened, she began to loiter among the daisies and buttercups. Sue kept well behind and out of sight – in the line of maples that edged the meadow. She hoped that Tabs would presently turn back, refreshed by her adventure, to forgive her cruel parent, and spend the rest of the day in contentment.

The hope seemed likely to be fulfilled, for Tabitha was now systematically picking daisies, and when her arms were filled, she looked around for a place to sit down and make a wreath – an accomplishment she had lately acquired. Then, just as Sue began to think of going back to the house, Tabitha put the daisies down beside the path and set off again.

The path, when it left the meadow, wandered through a grove of cedars and came out in a field behind Mona Stuart's studio barn, the roof of which was already visible.

From there the path straggled through a tangle of junipers and sweet fern, crossed a brook, and ultimately reached the highway, some distance away. Sue didn't think Tabitha would go beyond the brook – an entrancing spot to a child – and so didn't hurry in her pursuit, even when Tabitha disappeared among the cedars. The sun was burning Sue's shoulders through her thin cotton dress, and she was thankful when she, too, reached the cool, pungent shade.

Far ahead she saw Tabitha just emerging into the Stuart's back field, but there, instead of following the path, the small figure turned abruptly and made straight for the open door of the studio.

Oh heavens! Sue thought. She broke into a run, hoping to catch up with Tabitha before she reached the studio, rather than attract attention by shouting. She was too late. She was also too far behind to be present at her daughter's encounter with one of America's foremost artists, but she heard about it in detail for several days afterwards.

The studio was empty when Tabitha went in, and she made herself at home. At first she was astonished at the untidiness of the big, north-lighted room, lined with piled canvases. Then she saw the picture on the easel. It was one of Mona Stuart's finest – a study of sunlight on a meadow, its intensity so brilliant that the world seemed to swim a little beyond reality.

Tabitha was standing before it, her face ecstatic, when Mona Stuart appeared suddenly in the big double doorway.

'What are you doing here, little girl?'

'Running away,' said the artless Tabitha, her eyes still on the picture.

'Well, you can't run away here. Run somewhere else.'

Tabitha turned to her. 'I wasn't running away here. I just wanted to see.'

'Little girl,' said Mona Stuart, with ominous calm, 'will you either run away or go home – now! At once!'

Tabitha stared at her, wide-eyed. 'Oh!' she said. 'That's *rude*!'

'Rude?'

'Oh, yes.' Tabitha explained. 'Mummy says that no matter how much you don't want somebody around, you shouldn't say so. *Awful* people come to our house, and I never say a *word*.'

Tabitha was surprised by Mrs Stuart's sudden fit of coughing.

'I didn't mean to be rude,' Mona Stuart said, 'but what do you want to see here?'

'Oh. Well, I just wanted to see what was inside, but now I'm here I want to see this picture.'

'You do? Why?'

'Because,' Tabitha said, seriously, 'it's perfectly beautiful. It's the sunshine, I think. There's more than outside.'

The picture was to be called 'Light in July', and Mona Stuart looked at Tabitha with respect.

'Hm,' she said. 'Would you like to see some of the others?'

Sue heard this question as she paused in the back doorway. Sue saw Tabitha's delighted face turned up to Mona Stuart's. Neither of them was aware of Sue, who perceived that, despite Tabitha's unforgivable intrusion, an adjustment had been made, and she hesitated to interrupt with her own uninvited presence. It would be better to wait unobtrusively until Tabitha had been dismissed.

She stepped to one side and sat down under a lilac bush, while her small daughter was accorded a privilege recently denied the art critic of a New York newspaper, and the editor of a nationally circulated picture magazine. Tabitha was permitted a preview of Mona Stuart's autumn showing.

It was a highly successful preview. Mona Stuart was a truly distinguished artist, her work had simplicity as well as infinitely skilled complexity, and there was hardly a picture in which Tabitha did not find something to delight her. She missed the subtleties, of course, but she was thrilled by the brilliant colours and the rhythmic lines which gave depth and movement to the simplest studies. Even when she disapproved – 'I don't like those houses. They're sad –' Mrs Stuart gave a grunt of satisfaction.

'That's *beautiful*!' Tabitha would breathe, confronted by a jewel-coloured still life. Or, examining a half-completed sketch of the valley, 'Ooh, look at the wind blowing!'

When the last canvas had been returned to its place, Mona Stuart remarked suddenly, 'Aren't you Tabitha Barry?'

'Yes, I am. And you're Cal's mother. I knew as soon as you came in. But you don't seem like a mother. You don't take care of Cal, do you?'

There was a slight pause. Then Mona Stuart replied pleasantly, 'Cal's a good deal older than you. She doesn't need to be looked after.'

'But she says you didn't when she was little. Why didn't you?'

To Sue's astonishment, Mona Stuart replied seriously, 'Because Cornelia could do it better. I have to paint pictures.'

Tabitha glanced at the pictures glowing about her.

'Yes,' she acknowledged, 'I can see that. But Mummy

says that looking after your children is the most important thing in the world.'

Mrs Stuart's 'Hm,' sounded disconcerted, and Sue remembered how often she had, herself, become involved in a discussion with Tabitha, only to find herself so on the defensive that she wondered if Tabitha was going to be a lawyer.

'Looking after children,' Mona Stuart was saying, 'is something that should be done well, and I'm sure your mother is very good at it. But I wouldn't be. Cornelia is better.'

'I don't think so. It's not like having a mother.'

'Cal,' Mrs Stuart said flatly, 'wouldn't agree with you.'

Tabitha's reply brought Sue to her feet with a bound.

'Oh, but Cal *would*,' the clear little voice stated inexorably. 'She loves Cornelia, but she hates not having a real mother. She's always wishing she had one like ours. We have a wonderful mo –'

Sue stepped through the studio door to encounter two pairs of startled eyes.

'Tabs,' she said quietly, 'you shouldn't be here and you know it.' She turned to Mona Stuart. 'I'm so sorry about this intrusion. I'll see that it doesn't happen again.'

'That's perfectly all right,' Mona Stuart said. 'You've been very good to Cal. I hope she hasn't been a pest.'

'Far from it – she's been a great help. We all love her. Tabs, dear, will you say good-bye?'

'Good-bye,' Tabitha said obediently, 'I had a very nice time.'

She looked up at Sue, Mona Stuart forgotten. 'Mummy, will you hug me?'

'Of course I will, darling.' Sue dropped to one knee with an apologetic glance at Mrs Stuart. Tabitha flung herself into the welcoming arms.

'Mummy,' she said, with desperate honesty, 'I was running away, but now I'm not. Are you glad?'

'I'm very glad,' Sue told her. 'Were you mad at me, Tabs?'

Tabitha considered a button on her mother's dress, while Mona Stuart watched with frank interest.

'Not exactly at you,' Tabitha said, finally.

'Well, then, what made you so cross?'

Tabitha clung to Sue's hand, struggling for honesty and accuracy.

'I – I woke up that way,' she said at last, her forehead wrinkling. 'I sort of hurt in my thoughts, but it wasn't *about* anything. I was mad inside *me*. That's queer, isn't it?'

'Not really,' Sue reassured her. 'Everybody has times like that, and it's horrid. Did you feel better, running away?'

'Oh, yes! And then I saw those beautiful, *beautiful* pictures, and Cal's mother was good to me, and then you came. I feel fine.'

She smiled at Sue, who smiled back, and turned to Mona Stuart.

'I hope you'll forgive me for going into this just here.'

'What? Oh – why certainly.' She looked dumpy and tired.

Once outside the studio, Sue had intended to discuss further the matter of running away, going into places where one had not been invited, and interfering with other people's business. But before she could begin Tabitha cried eagerly, 'Oh look! Here comes Cal. She must've been at our house!'

Cal was running across the field, her short suit a yellow streak against the summer green.

'Oh, Mrs Barry!' she called. 'I've been looking for you

everywhere!' She bounded to a stop beside them, squeezed Tabitha, and flung an impulsive arm around Sue's waist. 'Were you in the studio? Did you meet Mother?'

'Just for a second, Tabitha barged in on her very rudely. We're on our way home.'

'Oh, good! Are you going to show me how to make a bed with a patient in it?'

'As soon as we get home,' Sue promised, taking Tabitha's hand and dropped her other arm across Cal's shoulders. 'Come on, kids. How would you like to make a big freezer of ice cream at home, and then, this afternoon, borrow Ira Prouty's sailboat and everybody go sailing on the lake?'

Tabitha shrieked.

'Oh!' Cal cried. 'Oh, Mrs Barry! You're so *swell*!'

They moved along the path, laughing and excited, an affectionate and happy trio. None of them thought of looking back, so they did not see Mona Stuart standing in the doorway of the studio, staring after them with a very odd expression on her plain, usually inexpressive face.

10

A quiet morning

It was the next day that Miss Layton, the visiting nurse, came down with acute laryngitis.

'For heaven's sake!' said Sue into the telephone. 'How did you get laryngitis this time of year?'

'Search me,' Miss Layton croaked. 'I'm sorry this is such short notice. I hope you didn't have anything planned.'

'Only routine things,' Sue assured her. 'I'd love to take over.'

'Well, I ought to be back tomorrow.'

'That's all right. Don't worry.'

'Okay. Here's your list, unless there have been some new calls, which I doubt. Things are pretty quiet right now – thank goodness! You ought to have an easy day and quit early. First, there's your old friend, Mrs Ventress – scalded foot dressing – she's so fat, now, that she can't get out of the way of her own cooking. Then there's Jim Barnes' kid with rheumatic fever – general care. Martha Todd's hired girl gets the cast off her foot today, and Miss Hallet is due a shot for arthritis. The bottle is in the medicine cabinet in my office.'

Miss Layton's voice was rapidly becoming a whisper, but she managed to finish the list of patients, of which there were only a few.

Sue was humming when she returned to the breakfast table and Bill chuckled.

'The old fire-horse,' he said. 'I take it that Layton is sick.'

'Yes – lost her voice.'

'Much of a list?'

'No. It's more scattered than heavy. Bill, did you know that Miss Hallett is laid up again? Dr Rail in the village has started her on those new shots. Poor soul, I hope they work. What do you suppose she's living on? You can't give music lessons with arthritis.'

'I suspect the Todds are taking care of the financial angle.'

'You might know! Bless Martha! There's nothing like marrying money in your declining years. What a break that was – for all of us.'

They were both silent, thinking of the wiry, dynamic Martha Edgett and her sharp-tongued propensity for doing good. Elias Todd, the rich elderly owner of Bald Trail Inn, had fallen in love with her the night of a bad hurricane when everybody had taken refuge in the church. He was notorious for his caution, but before he had time for deliberation he was celebrating his marriage to Martha by giving Springdale a badly needed hospital.

Martha, he explained, had said that he should, and if Martha had said it, it must be right.

He had never regretted his faith in her – nor had anyone else – particularly those in trouble.

'It's extraordinary,' said Sue, thinking aloud, 'when you remember what a stuffed shirt Elias was before Martha got him.'

She had forgotten the listening children, and now, to her horror, Johnny inquired, 'What's a stuffed shirt?'

Bill disappeared behind his napkin.

'Ask your father,' said Sue promptly.

'What's a stuffed shirt, Daddy?'

Bill emerged from behind his napkin, gave Sue a highly expressive glance, cleared his throat, and said, 'Well – a – uh – a stuffed shirt means somebody who – uh – doesn't feel very well.'

Sue chanted under her breath, 'You can't get out of it that way!'

She was right, for Tabitha demanded instantly. 'What do you mean, Daddy? Was Uncle Elias sick?'

'Well – he had a slight problem, but you are not to mention it, nor ask him about it. He wouldn't like it.'

'But what *was* it, Daddy?'

Bill hesitated a fraction of a second and then pronounced rapidly. 'He had a superabundance of megalomania arising from excessive local prominence.'

'Oh!' said the stunned Tabitha and was silent.

Bill rose to leave. 'I hope that'll larn you,' he muttered to the convulsed Sue.

When he had gone she hurried upstairs to change into her blue uniform. Tabitha followed to admire, for the uniform, to Tabitha, was not only a thing of beauty, but an insignia of great importance.

'What'll we do while you're gone, Mummy?' Tabs worried. 'It's horrid when you're away.'

'I'm sorry, darling, but I have to go. Cal will probably be over later, and you'll like that.'

'No, I won't,' said Tabitha obstinately. 'I don't like to be *here* when you're gone.'

'Then why don't you and the boys go over to the Bonneys'? You always have fun there, and Cherry will look after you. Maybe you could get Cal to go with you.'

'All right,' said Tabitha, cheered. 'Do you think Cherry would let me hold the baby? I wish *we* had a baby, Mummy. Why don't we? I'd take *all* the care of it.'

'Would you indeed?' said Sue, smiling.

She checked over her Henry Street bag, which was always ready in the downstairs hall closet, told Veazie Ann that the children were going to the Bonneys', kissed the three woebegone little faces, and with Maxl at her heels went out the back door to start the station wagon.

She had just lifted Maxl in, and was turning the car when she saw the dumpy, white-coated figure of Mona Stuart tramping up the lane. 'What on earth? And at this hour, too.'

Mona Stuart put her head in through the open car window, and, wasting no words on the weather or the state of Sue's health, said:

'I want to talk to you about Cal, Mrs Barry. If you're in a hurry I'll go away, but I'd like to come back.'

Sue explained that she was relieving for the visiting nurse and must check in at the hospital. 'But I have two calls back this way. Why don't you drive down with me? I won't be a minute in the hospital.'

'Thank you,' said Mona Stuart and climbed into the station wagon. She said nothing more until the car was out of the lane and headed down the mountain. Then she began:

'Your little girl said some things yesterday which gave me a pretty bad night. She thinks that Cal is unhappy, and that it's my fault. Do you think so?'

Sue didn't attempt a tactful reply. Whatever this woman's shortcomings, she was starkly honest and she deserved an honest answer.

'Cal isn't unhappy in the exact sense of the word, Mrs Stuart. She's confused, and very much off on the wrong foot.'

'Seriously so?'

'Yes.'

'Is it my fault?'

Sue hesitated. After all, she couldn't be sure whose fault it was. She had only heard one side of the story.

'Frankly,' she said, 'I don't know enough about it to answer that question.'

'Well – what's wrong?'

Sue considered for a long minute, distressed by the sudden responsibility thrust upon her and only too aware of the dangers of meddling with other people's lives. When she spoke it was with care.

'Cal,' she said, 'is obsessed with the idea that her beauty is a barrier between herself and the world – that no one is interested in her as a person. My husband thinks it's tied up with her feeling that she's not important to you; that you don't love her.'

Mona Stuart gave a faint gasp.

Sue waited, her eyes on the road, and presently the voice beside her said harshly, 'Thank you for not beating about the bush. I do love Cal, and she is important to me. What should I do?'

'I think,' said Sue, 'that the trouble lies, not in the amount of time and attention you've given Cal, but in the *kind* of attention you've given her. You've been busy, and naturally rather detached. Children don't understand detachment. It seems to them a form of rejection. Cal needs to think that you are actively interested in her – that you understand how she feels, and care about it.'

'But I haven't the faintest idea how Cal feels. I'm not very good with people, you see. I watched you yesterday with your little girl, and then with Cal, so I think I understand what you mean. I wouldn't know how to apply it.'

'Oh dear!' said Sue.

'Exactly. If Cal's father had lived things might have been different. He had the same kind of perception you seem to have. But he died two months before Cal was born, and I've never known what to do with her, or about her. I – I thought Cornelia was the solution.'

'Why don't you talk to Cornelia about it. She'd know better than anyone how you could give Cal what she needs.'

'Hm. Maybe you're right.'

They went on down the hill in silence and had just reached the last turn when Mrs Stuart said, 'I'd like to think this over, and I believe I'll walk back – if you'll just let me out here.'

'Certainly.'

Sue stopped the car. The dumpy figure started back up the hill – her slip showing. She had not once thought of suggesting that Sue visit her, or that there was any likelihood of their ever meeting again – a simple unawareness which explained a great deal, but was not too hopeful for Cal.

Sue drove on through the village. She would have liked to give more attention to the problem of Mona Stuart and Cal, but she had work to do and the habit of years turned her mind into old channels. She began to plan her day.

Since she needn't drive Mrs Stuart home it would be more practical to put in the morning on the cases in the village. If she finished them before lunch and no further calls came in, she could have lunch at home. There would be only the plaster cast and Miss Hallett for the afternoon, and both patients were on her own road.

She bounced across the bridge over the little river and turned the car up the mountain road to the hospital on the bluff. Since Kit had been gone Sue had not been in the hospital. It was strange to think of the place without Kit, whose brief and cheerful letters from home made no mention of her return.

Sue didn't know the nursing faculty very well now. There had been changes through the years, and old friends who had spent much time at Sue's house had been replaced by strangers. In her capacity as Bill's wife she invited them for tea or dinner occasionally, but otherwise she saw little of them.

The gravel spurted under her tyres as she put on her brakes in the hospital driveway and parked near the entrance. She ran lightly up the steps and opened the door, sniffing the familiar hospital smell.

'Hello, Gerty,' she said to the telephone operator, who beamed and hurriedly removed her headphones.

'Sakes! Mrs Barry! At it again? It's been kind of a while, seem's as though.'

'Oh, it's not so long,' said Sue defensively. 'I was relieving last November – that's no time at all. It's nice to see you, Gerty. How's your mother?'

'Raising Cain as usual,' said Gerty, whose mother was an extremely disagreeable old lady.

'That's too bad. I know it's hard for you. Can't you get her to visit her sister for a while?'

'Not if she thinks I want it. There's nothing come in for you, Mrs Barry. We ain't even had a good drowneding since I dunno when.'

Sue laughed and went on into Miss Layton's office where she collected Miss Hallett's bottle and then stood thinking of Gerty's first remark. It troubled her. Even Gerty thought it had been 'kind of a while' since Sue had done any real nursing – and it had. Was it a mistake?

'I wish,' Sue muttered, 'that I'd stop worrying about this, unless I'm going to do something about it.'

Well, she had something to do about it right now, and she'd better be about it. She left the hospital a few minutes later, bracing herself for the vigorous, fourteen-stone Mrs Ventress, who, once started talking was difficult to stop.

She proved, in fact, impossible to stop, and Sue dressed the badly scalded foot without having a chance to utter a single world. Mrs Ventress's double chins wobbled and her voice went on and on.

'Stars alive, Mrs Barry! Seems like old times to have you a-making the rounds but I guess you ain't lost your old touch, though most any touch is liable to – OUCH! I didn't mean to jump but my nerves ain't what they was – not that I ain't always been delicate – no real strength in me. I was saying to Tom the other day, s'I, I ain't seen hide nor hair of Mrs Barry in a dog's age, but a husband and three children is dretful hard on a woman. OUCH! That foot's a sight, ain't it? But we ain't none of us forgot all you and the doctor done for us in the hurricane. Land! Remember that awful time we had with the typhoid fever? Though I've heard tell they've got something for it now. Land! I dunno what they'll think of next! And all that about my ice cream and Lot Phinney's dog, the pesky critter, and now he's sold the old Irwin place to that crazy artist woman and some says she smokes seegars and paints people in the – in the – altogether. I don't hold with such goings on and I says so to Lot, but he's such a cantankerous old coot! Why, one time –'

Sue got away at last, pursued still by Mrs Ventress's voice, and carrying a bag of frosted cupcakes for the children.

At Jim Barnes' her welcome was equally enthusiastic but far less garrulous and again Sue felt a vague stirring of guilt. She bathed the feverish little boy, made him laugh with stories of the twins, and departed with two dozen ears of corn, a lemon, a lemon pie, and the fervent good wishes of the child's mother.

'Goodness knows, Mrs Barry, I wish't we had more to give you. Billy ain't laughed like that sence he was took down. We miss you, Mrs Barry, all of us, here in the village.'

By the time Sue had finished with her village calls and was ready to go home for lunch the back of the station wagon was piled with awkwardly presented loaves of home-made bread, boxes of fresh berries, new-laid eggs, a dressed chicken, and a bottle of elderberry wine. Maxl glared indignantly from the midst of the confusion.

Sue turned the car homeward, feeling tired and depressed.

Oh, I don't know, she thought. It seems to me I'm doing the best I can – but very likely I'm not. I could do more nursing, now that the twins are so much older.

She looked for the children as she turned up the lane. They were not in the yard – but, of course, they were having lunch. She paused in the garden to pick the head off a dead marigold and then, going in through the kitchen to get a basket for the things in the car, she found Veazie Ann busy at the stove and the house silent.

'Where are the kids?' she asked. 'Did Cal come over?'

'Just for a minute, but she didn't stay. She wouldn't go to the Bonneys'. Tabs and Johnny are having lunch there. Jerry's upstairs. He wouldn't go.'

'For Pete's sake! Why not?'

'Well, after you left he started that bong-bonging, and when Tabs undertook to boss him he had a spell. So they went along and I tried to calm him down. 'Twasn't what you'd call a considerable success, especially with Johnny gone.'

'How is he now?'

'Quieter – on account of he's wore out. 'Tain't a calm quiet. I always figures there wasn't a young one I couldn't manage, but what ails Jerry beats me.'

Sue went upstairs.

Jerry was sitting moodily on the nursery floor spinning the wheels of a tiny jeep which he held in his hands. He was tear-stained and blotched and, to the accompaniment of a dreary, rhythmic humming, was bumping the back of his head against the wall.

'Well, how's my boy?' said Sue brightly.

Jerry stared at her. Then his face puckered. He flung the jeep across the room and began to roar.

Oh-oh! Sue thought. The fresh audience! I should have stayed downstairs and made exciting noises. It was too late for that now, however, so she knelt and put her arms around him.

'Jerry,' she began quietly.

Jerry turned a brick red, broke away from her, and rolled screaming under his bed.

It was impossible to be tender with someone who was screaming under a bed. Sue changed her tactics.

'That's enough, Jerry! Stop it, and tell me what's the matter!'

The only answer was a drumming of heels on the floor and louder howls.

'*Jerry!*'

'Waa-a-a-aaaAAAAH!'

Oh Lord! Sue thought wearily. If he could only be reasoned with like Tabs, or left alone like Johnny, but he just goes on and on and on. She reached down, and, seizing him by the foot, pulled him, fighting and squalling, from under the bed.

'Jerry! Jerry!' She held him close in an effort to give him a feeling of warmth and safety, but he only fought to

escape. Sue considered the standard remedy for hysterics –
cold water. But she couldn't see herself throwing cold
water in Jerry's frantic little face, even if it were for his
own good. He must be hideously tired, anyway, and a
sudden shock seemed unfair.

She picked him up, avoiding his heels, and put him on
his bed. When he made no attempt to get up she drew a
light blanket over him. He was still sobbing, but when
she bent to kiss him his arms went around her neck and
clung. This tantrum would end, she knew, like all the
others – in exhausted sleep, after which he would behave
as if nothing had happened.

She left him there and went slowly downstairs, wondering how she could possibly have been thinking, an
hour ago, that the nursing profession couldn't get along
without her, and her children could.

11

Miss Hallett discovers

Sue and Veazie Ann had lunch on the back screened porch where they could look out at the hill pasture swimming in the heat. The meal was embellished with some of the home-made bread and large bowls of raspberries and cream, but Sue was too troubled to enjoy it. She wished, fretfully, that she could take off her girdle and stockings. A midsummer noon in the White Mountains could be just as hot as anywhere else – hotter when it chose, and it did choose.

She drank three glasses of iced tea, grateful for the coolness, and was just about to suggest that Veazie Ann give Jerry some lemonade after his nap, when she heard the clump of his sandals in the kitchen. That was too bad. He needed more than half an hour's sleep.

He appeared on the screened porch looking crumpled and hot but reasonably at peace.

'Come here, baby,' said Sue, and he came, to lean confidingly against her. She kissed the flushed little face. 'Goodness, but you're sticky! Why don't you go barefooted, dear? And get out of those roasting overalls. You don't need anything but a sun suit.'

'All right,' said Jerry, and promptly stripped to the skin. Then, pink and naked, he climbed into Sue's lap.

'Want some raspberries?' Sue asked.

'Yes.'

'Yes, what?'

'Yes, please.'

Veazie Ann rose. 'I'll get them, Sue. And a nice cold washcloth, too.'

Sue wiped Jerry's face and hands and he ate the raspberries – languidly – and drank a glass of milk. He was still very tired, but Sue knew that there would be no more nap today. Why not take him with her ? The Todds would be delighted, and Miss Hallett was used to children. The ride and change would rest him, and Veazie Ann could have a quiet afternoon.

'Do him good,' Veazie Ann agreed. 'They've got some new puppies over at Todds', and there never was a young one wasn't the better for the sight of a mess of puppies.'

'Want to come with me, darling ?'

Jerry nodded, and leaned back against Sue, but he had brightened at the word 'puppies'.

Sue telephoned the hospital to see if any calls had come in, but none had. She put Jerry into a blue-and-white-checked sun suit, inspected his fingernails, and they set off.

It was cooler driving, for most of the road was in shade, and presently Jerry began to sing 'Twinkle, Twinkle, Little Star'. He sang all four verses, over and over – all the way to the Todds, and Sue perceived that she had been wise to bring him. She would, however, after the first ten or fifteen minutes, have appreciated a change of song.

The Todds lived in a big, remodelled farmhouse, roomy and comfortable and cool. Behind it were Elias Todd's dachshund kennels, long since removed from the grounds of the fashionable Bald Trail Inn, of which Elias was still owner, though no longer manager. It was to the kennels that the adoring Martha led Jerry, while Sue stayed behind to tackle the maid's plaster cast.

She smiled, watching them go. Martha Todd was as wiry and energetic as on the day, years ago, when she had discovered Sue, forlorn and discouraged, sitting on a rock beside the road – and had changed the world for her. Jerry pattered along beside Martha, his red curls shining in the sun, and his freckled face turned up in a glow of anticipation. Whatever his problem, it was forgotten now.

Sue went upstairs to the maid's room.

'Well, Effie,' she said, to the robust-looking girl on the couch, 'if I take that thing off your ankle, will you promise not to fall through another ladder?'

'You bet I will, Mrs Barry! That cast's hotter than Job's boils.'

It was an hour before Sue and Jerry left the Todds, one filled with iced tea, the other with root-beer. The heavy shadow of the mountain lay upon the road now, and Jerry stood up all the way to Miss Hallett's, luxuriating in the cooler wind. He chattered incessantly about the puppies which he had christened Florio, Morio, Dorio, and Korio, although he was not sure which was which. The tired Sue listened, happy to hear him.

Miss Hallett's little yellow cottage stood back from the road, half buried in syringa and azalea bushes. A double line of hollyhocks flanked the path to the door.

'Do you want to stay in the car, or play around in the yard?' Sue asked.

'Oh, the yard! And –' virtuously – 'I won't go in the road or pick any of the flowers.'

'I'm delighted to hear it,' said his mother, and left him running about the azalea bushes.

She knocked on the screen door.

'Come in,' Miss Hallett called.

Sue went through the kitchen to the sunny living-room,

pleasant with its ruffled curtains, rag rugs, and upright piano. She was shocked to find Miss Hallett in a wheel chair, her swollen hands, once so quick and true, lying motionless in her lap. It was a brutal last blow in life which had been one long frustration, for Miss Hallett had been a brilliant pianist who had given up a concert career on the death of her sister, to come home and support her mother by giving music lessons to bored and rebellious children. Now even that had been taken away.

'Why, Sue!' Miss Hallett exclaimed. Her thin, lined face beneath the white hair was bright with pleasure. 'This is the nicest surprise I've had in a long while!'

She caught sight of Jerry through the window.

'Oh, you've brought the twins! Can't they come in? I haven't seen them since they were toddlers.'

'I only brought Jerry with me,' Sue said, hating herself for not having come to see Miss Hallett more often. She went to the door and called Jerry, who ran eagerly to the house but greeted Miss Hallet with a subdued murmur.

'Hello, there,' said Miss Hallett. 'This is a very nice visit.'

Jerry stared, momentarily at a loss. Then he glanced around the room and fixed his attention on the piano.

'What's that big, funny thing?' he demanded.

'Why, it's a piano,' said the astonished Miss Hallett. 'Haven't you ever seen one?'

'No, thank you. What does it do?'

'It makes music.'

'How?'

'He's a child of the machine age,' said Sue, laughing. 'He thinks music comes out of the gramophone or the radio.'

'You mean you don't have a *piano*?' said the shocked Miss Hallett.

'What would we do with one? Bill used to play a little, but he hasn't touched a piano since he was in college. I studied faithfully for two years when I was a child, and in the end I could play "The Happy Farmer" and absolutely nothing else. I played "The Happy Farmer" dutifully, until my father decided he could be driven crazy in cheaper ways. And nobody in the neighbourhood has a piano, so it's all new to Jerry.'

'How does it work, please?' said Jerry.

Sue went over to the piano and struck a few notes. 'Like that,' she said.

Jerry was charmed. 'Can I do it? Can I do it?'

'Of course you may,' Miss Hallett told him, and then, noticing Sue's dubious expression, 'Don't worry, Sue. It's a tough old piano, and friendly to children.'

Jerry climbed up on the piano stool, and after a tentative poke or two at the keys began, like all children, to bang haphazardly.

'Where shall we go to give you your shot?' Sue asked, raising her voice above the din.

'My bedroom is just off the kitchen. Mother has my old one upstairs.'

'How is your mother? I was just going to ask you where she is.'

'She's upstairs resting. You know, Sue, it's remarkable – she's eighty-three, but she nips around like a girl – and looks after me much better than any girl could do.'

Miss Hallett was wheeling herself across to the door as she spoke, refusing Sue's offer of help. 'I like to do as much as I can for myself,' she explained. 'Actually, I don't walk too badly, but this is easier and quicker when I have a bad day.'

Sue's hypodermic syringe was already sterile, so the injection was a matter of moments. After it, she and Miss

Hallett sat on the edge of the big, four-poster bed, talking, while Jerry banged away at the piano.

Miss Hallett listened to him and laughed. 'He's played all the white notes,' she said, 'and now he's playing all the black ones. Children invariably do that.'

She was silent for a moment and then asked, 'Sue, do you think these shots will really do anything for me? Doctors are so vague.'

Sue told her as much as she herself knew, describing the inexplicable complete cures, and the equally inexplicable failures. It was some time before she re-established Miss Hallett in the wheel chair and returned with her to the living-room.

Jerry was still at the piano.

'Come on, fella,' said Sue. 'It's time to go home.'

'Oh, no, Mummy! *Please!*'

Sue would have been firm on any other day, but now she turned apologetically to Miss Hallett.

'Do you mind if I ease him along for a few minutes? He's had a very h-a-r-d d-a-y.'

'By all means,' Miss Hallett said. 'I like to hear him. You'd be surprised how much I miss the children – especially the little ones. By the way, I understand there's a new baby in the Bonney family. Another child is always welcome there.'

They discussed the village news for a time, and then Sue noticed that Miss Hallett was becoming more and more aware of Jerry and the piano – and no wonder! All that noise must be getting on her nerves. Sue rose decisively.

'We really must go,' said Sue. Miss Hallett didn't seem to hear.

'I think we'd better be going,' Sue repeated, raising her voice a little. 'I've enjoyed this so much, and I hope that you'll –'

'Hush!' said Miss Hallett.

She was listening to Jerry with startled attention, and suddenly wheeled herself over to the piano.

Sue followed, wondering.

Jerry was striking single notes with one finger, and his mother, watching, saw that starting with middle C he was playing the first, third and fifth notes up, and then playing all five down, stopping again on middle C. He was striking the notes rhythmically, and the pattern of sound stirred a vague memory in Sue. It had something to do with chords – but what?

The voice of her own music teacher came to her across the years, a voice saying with hopeless patience: 'No, no. You play the chord in a little tune, Sue – like this: Trot! Trot! Trot! Trot my pony, trot!'

Jerry, however, couldn't possibly know it.

'Wait a minute, Jerry,' Miss Hallett said. He paused obediently and she struck the same notes with one swollen finger, but stopped before middle C.

'Why,' she said to Jerry, 'didn't *you* stop there?'

He looked at her, surprised. 'It wouldn't be right,' he said, seriously.

'Why not?'

'Because it *has* to go back,' Jerry explained, impatient with grown-up stupidity.

'It does indeed,' Miss Hallett returned in an odd tone. 'Jerry – these black and white things are the piano keys, but we call them notes, and you are quite right – every song has one note where it's happiest. We call it the home note. It's like a nest for little birds. They all fly out from it, but they always come back to it.'

She turned to Sue. 'What song does he know?' she asked.

' "Twinkle, Twinkle, Little Star",' Sue answered automatically.

'Splendid!' Miss Hallett played it with one finger.

'Let me! Let me!' Jerry shouted, his eyes shining. He played it without hesitation.

Miss Hallet's eyes, too, were shining.

'Jerry,' she said, striking the D next to middle C, 'could you play it from here?'

He tried, and began to breathe hard – a sure sign that he was losing his temper.

'Sometimes you have to use a black note,' Miss Hallett said quietly.

He fumbled, struck the F sharp at last, and went on.

'Try it somewhere else – anywhere.'

Sue listened, amused, while 'Twinkle, Twinkle, Little Star' was played from one end of the piano to the other. It was played hesitantly, with a great deal of searching among the black notes, but it was always recognizable, and always ended with a flourish.

Miss Hallett looked up at Sue. 'He's found the home note,' she said, 'in every single key.'

Sue nodded, pleased. Her knowledge of musical technicalities was too slight for her to attach any significance to the statement, beyond the realization that Miss Hallett considered Jerry smart.

'But don't most children –' Sue was beginning, when she perceived that Miss Hallett was starting Jerry off on 'Jingle Bells'.

Sue waited patiently as long as she could, thankful to see Jerry so relaxed, but somewhat surprised by it, for, as she well remembered, a piano could be the most maddening thing in the world. Nevertheless, the afternoon was wearing on.

'Jerry,' she said at last, 'it's very good of Miss Hallett to let you do this, but we really –'

'Just a minute, Sue,' Miss Hallett said, sharply. 'Jerry,

what else did you find out about the piano when we were
in the other room?'

Jerry paused.

'Well,' he said. 'Things match. Like this.' He struck
E and C together, with two forefingers. 'And way up
here –' he was suddenly tense – 'I found something better!
It's the best of all! Mummy said I couldn't but I can!'

He struck an F sharp and G sharp alternately, trying to
drum on them in a stumbling semblance of a trill.

'The rain!' he shouted. 'I *can* make it rain! I can! I can!
You said I couldn't, Mummy, but I *can*!'

Miss Hallett reached out and played the trill smoothly
though she winced with pain, and Jerry cried, 'Yes! Yes!
See, Mummy?'

Sue laughed. 'I see, darling. I didn't understand before.
I thought you wanted to make the rain *fall*.'

'Oh, no, Mummy. It was the noise.' He turned back
to the piano.

'What happened?' Miss Hallett asked, and while Jerry
worked on, oblivious, Sue told Miss Hallett the story of
the rain, the church bells, and the pickle fork.

'I understand about the pickle fork,' Sue finished,
'because I'd said the drops on the window looked like
silver, and Jerry wanted to know whether silver made a
noise. So I got him a silver fork and it did make a noise,
but I didn't understand that he was trying to find something that would make the *sound* of rain. Anyway, why
couldn't he have drummed with his fingers?'

'Because he heard the rain as a musical note – not just
beating.'

'Oh! Well, whatever it was, he wound up with a most
ghastly tantrum.'

'I'm sure he did,' said Miss Hallett dryly. 'Does he
have many tantrums?'

'He's beginning to, but they aren't usually about anything, as that one was.'

'If you'll forgive an old woman's impertinence, Sue, I'd say they were about something very important, and the sooner you get him a piano the better.'

'A *piano*! But he's only four and a half years old!'

'That, my dear, is a good deal of the point. I've heard about this sort of thing, but this is the first time I've ever seen it. Jerry has incredible talent, Sue. He's almost – well, really, I hardly know *what* to say.'

Sue stared at Miss Hallett. Jerry's bangings on the piano had not seemed to her in any way out of the ordinary – merely a small boy's pleased experiments with a new toy.

'But,' she said, bewildered, 'he was only picking out simple tunes with one finger – after you'd showed him. Don't most children –'

Miss Hallett shook her head. 'He was doing much more than that, Sue. Any older child with a good ear could have played them, given a little time, but at Jerry's age only a born musician could do it instantly – as he did. He has an instinctive feeling for the home note, and for chords in every key. Remember, he's never seen a piano before. It's as though he'd been born with all harmony and the entire keyboard in his head.'

Sue turned uncertainly to look at Jerry. 'I don't know what to say either,' she told Miss Hallett. 'Was – is that what's been wrong with him? I mean his restlessness and all those tantrums.'

'I think so.'

'Well, it's a relief to know that, but what do we do with him now?'

'Just get him a piano and let his musical development take its course.'

Sue considered this with anything but enthusiasm. Then she said, 'I don't want to hold him back, Miss Hallett, but I don't want to force him either. He's too little to be made to practise for hours and sweat over music lessons. I want him to grow up a normal, happy boy, doing all the things other children do. I don't want him to spend his childhood shackled to a piano, no matter how much talent he has.'

'Of course you don't – and he shouldn't. All he'll need for a time will be a piano and the sort of help I gave him today – a few minutes of suggestion and the rest left to him. If he seems to be spending too much time at the piano – send him out.'

This didn't sound very gruelling. Sue felt reassured, but she was still finding the news difficult to grasp. If only Bill were here too – she looked at Jerry. Talent or no talent, he was going to get down off that piano stool, so that his mother could go home to his father.

12

Tea with the Stuarts

BILL sat down on the back steps, the garden hose dangling and dripping from his hand.

'Are you kidding?' he asked.

'I am not.' Sue dropped down beside him.

'For Pete's sake! Well, I suppose the old girl knows what she's talking about.' He glanced across the yard to the sand pile and grinned. 'The darned little cuss! How do you suppose it happened?'

'I wouldn't know. He certainly didn't get it from *me*. But even I can see – now that it's been pointed out to me – that he has talent and ought to have a piano.'

'Is it all right,' Bill inquired mildly, 'if he starts out in a small way? Or do I run down to the general store and pick him out a concert grand – that is, if I can find any loose change in my other pants.'

'We could rent one of those minipianos. You could get one in Winslow.'

'I'll save the receipted bills and make Jerry pay me back when he's earning big money. Does he get a black velvet suit with a lace collar?'

'Certainly. It'll be worth it to see his face when he's told to wear it. He thinks anything but dirty overalls is too fancy.'

'We can let his hair grow long, too. Luckily he won't need a permanent.'

Sue laughed and held out her hand. Bill's closed over it warmly.

'I feel better,' Sue told him.

They fell into a companionable silence, watching the children, until Sue remarked suddenly, 'When they're old enough to get married, they're going to hear plenty from me.'

'What, for instance?'

'Well – that it takes ages to make a good marriage – that the first raptures are an awful strain, so that you get on one another's nerves –'

'You mean that fish?'

'I mean that fish!'

They both laughed, remembering their first real quarrel, which now seemed incredible.

'Neither of us, today,' said Sue, 'could possibly misunderstand each other like that. That's what I mean – it takes time and knowing another person a long while.' She paused and then asked, 'Do I often annoy you?'

'You certainly do!' said Bill with feeling.

'Does it matter?'

'Not to me.'

'Same here. But lots of people don't know that. They're stuffed so full of talk about romantic love and palpitating for-ever-and-ever that they don't know that there's anything else to it.'

'That's right,' said Bill. 'The real thing comes with shared life and experience, and you can't have that until you've had it – if you follow me.'

'I do. But it takes years. I don't mean following you. I mean growing together.' She smiled at him. 'I've got to get organized and give the kids their baths. All I wanted to say was – it's been worth it.'

Bill rose with her, his arm warm about her as he kissed

her. 'It has, at that,' he said, and watched her go indoors.

Bill went to Winslow the next day and arranged to have the piano delivered, while Sue took the clamouring Jerry back to Miss Hallett, who urged her to leave him there for the morning. She promised to telephone the minute Jerry was tired.

This produced a very bleak state of mind in Johnny. He rebuffed all efforts to cheer him until he caught sight of Cal coming across the fields.

'Well,' said Sue, as Cal came up with Tabs and Johnny clinging to either hand. 'Where were you yesterday? All kinds of things were going on.'

'I suppose so,' said Cal, wearily. 'I didn't want to go to the Bonneys'. What happened? Did Cherry do something spectacular?'

'No, it had nothing to do with Cherry. But I do wish you'd go over and see her, Cal. She'd be friends with you in a minute if you'd let her.'

'I'd rather not, honestly, Mrs Barry. I guess Cherry's all right but I just *can't*! I – I've got trouble enough.'

Sue glanced at her quickly, and then sent the children for bottles of ginger ale and a plentiful supply of straws. Cal, however, seemed unaware that any opening for confidence had been made.

'What did happen?' Cal asked.

Sue told her about Jerry, and Cal listened, wide-eyed.

'My goodness!' she exclaimed, when Sue had finished. 'I should think you'd be *terribly* proud.'

'I am, in a way, I suppose, but it's a little disconcerting. And Cal – don't say anything about it. The less fuss the better for everybody – Jerry included.'

Cal nodded, and then, to Sue's surprise, the girl's lips quivered.

'Oh!' Cal burst out, passionately, 'you're just wonderful! You're always thinking about what's best for everybody but yourself!'

'Now wait a minute,' Sue began crisply, but before she could finish the children appeared with bottles and straws and a bag of cookies. Cal ran to meet them.

Something, Sue was positive, had happened between Cal and her mother, or Cal would never have exploded like that. However there didn't seem much that could be done about it at the moment. The children were begging Cal to come on an expedition to the birch grove at the top of the hill pasture. Cal, after a shy, apologetic glance at Sue, agreed.

In the kitchen Veazie Ann was putting up blueberries, and Sue was helping her put a fresh half dozen jars in the pressure cooker when they heard a step on the porch.

'May I come in, Mrs Barry?' Cornelia said. 'Good morning, Mrs Cooney. I see you-all are into it, sure enough.'

'Land, yes,' Veazie Ann said. 'And we're going to have a scorcher, too. Must've been hotter than Tophet coming across that field. Sue – there's a pitcher of iced tea in the refrigerator.'

'Oh, good!' Sue put down the bowl of berries she was picking over. 'Do come in, Cornelia.'

'Excuse me, Mrs Barry. Miss Mona sent me to ask if you and the children would have tea with her tomorrow afternoon – with her and Cal. And she sends her apologies for not calling on you herself, but she's been right busy.'

Sue grinned inwardly. She doubted very much if Mrs Stuart had made any excuses whatsoever, or was even aware that the custom of sending one's employees to deliver invitations had gone out with the institution of rural free delivery, and the invention of the telephone.

'Thank you very much, Cornelia,' she said. 'We'd love to come. And now you're here, do stop a minute. I'll bring the iced tea outside, where we can get a little breeze. How about you, Veazie Ann?'

'Oh, you go on. I'll keep a'goin' as I be, I guess. Once I git started, I can't abide to stop.'

Sue carried the iced tea out to the little table under the elms, established Cornelia in a lawn chair, and sat down, thankful to be out of the hot kitchen.

'This is better!' she exclaimed, lifting her face to the breeze from across the valley. 'Cal and the children have gone up the hill in all this heat – and I doubt if they even notice it. How does Cal seem to you, Cornelia? I've helped her as much as I could – but I don't think I've been very successful.'

'You've done a lot for her, Mrs Barry. Some ways she's happier than I've ever seen her. But right now – well, to tell the truth, Mrs Barry, Miss Mona's kind of mixing things up.'

'Oh, no!' said Sue, involuntarily.

'Yes'm. She told me what you said, and I'm right glad you said it, Mrs Barry. But it's going to take a while, I reckon. She tried with Cal, all day yesterday, but all she knew to do was ask the child questions, one after the other, like a policeman.'

'Good heavens! How did Cal take it?'

'Cal don't like it at all. She don't know what to make of it, and she's kind of half scared and half mad. She don't say anything to me – but I know. So I had to tell Miss Mona she was doing it all wrong and too sudden, and poor Miss Mona, she looked so blue I had to think of something. It was me had the notion for this tea-party.'

Sue nodded. 'I thought probably.'

'Yes'm. I said to Miss Mona, I said "If you-all want

Cal to feel you're interested in her, just you ask her friends here. She ain't never had any of her friends in her own house," I told her. "You invite Mrs Barry and the children and you talk and be nice, and pay attention, like you was interested because they're Cal's friends." '

'Cornelia, you're a darling,' said Sue, heartily, realizing more than ever that, had Mona Stuart listened to Cornelia earlier, this situation would never have existed. 'Does Cal know?'

'Not yet. She'd already started for here when I got the notion.'

'Well, it's a good one. I don't see what can go wrong. There'll just be me and the children.' Sue stared for a moment at the clinking ice in her glass. Then she said slowly, 'Cornelia, can't you just *tell* Cal flatly that her mother loves her and is trying to tell her so?'

'It wouldn't make sense to her, Mrs Barry. Miss Mona's been blind too long, and the child's been too bad hurt by it. Besides, she's the wrong age.'

'Wrong a – Oh! You mean if she were younger she'd be more adaptable, and if she were older she'd be able to understand her mother better?'

'Yes'm. That's about it. Words wouldn't do any good right now.'

Cornelia paused and finished her tea. 'Well, I reckon I'd better go along back. Miss Mona's working and she don't have right good sense, those times. The house could burn over her head. My *goodness*! I reckon I ain't built right for getting out of lawn chairs. You've been real kind, Mrs Barry. I thank you.'

Sue returned languidly to the house, thinking that if a thunderstorm didn't turn up to cool the air before to-morrow the tea-party – far from being a gala occasion – would resemble a ward full of sleeping-sickness cases.

The storm materialized, however, late that afternoon, just as Bill got back from Winslow with the news that Jerry's piano would be delivered in a day or two. Sue had just finished telling him about Mona Stuart's invitation when the storm struck, and in the general dash to close windows, get the children indoors, and convince Johnny that his pet frog would rather be out than in, the Stuart situation was forgotten.

Sue didn't get around to telling the children about the invitation until the next day. They were delighted – particularly Tabitha, who felt that she already had entré into the Stuart's home.

'Wear your white dress, Mummy,' Tabitha said firmly. 'You're terribly pretty in it, and I want you to look nice.'

'All right, darling. Anything else?'

'No,' Tabitha said, kindly, 'I guess that's all.'

They took the road to the Stuarts', this time, instead of going over the pastures, in deference to Tabitha's sprigged percale and the twins' impeccable navy shorts and white shirts.

'You'll love the pictures, Mummy,' Tabitha said. 'They're the most –'

'No, Tabs,' Sue said quickly. 'You are not to ask to see the pictures or even mention them.'

'But why?' asked the bewildered Tabitha. 'She showed me the pictures herself. She wanted to.'

'Yes, but she may not want to show them again. Let's not get any extra strain into this tea-party.'

Tabitha looked up, ready to demand explanations, but was awed into silence on being confronted by the unfamiliar doorway with its polished eagle knocker.

Cal let them in, looking very cool and lovely in a green linen dress, but after her first, spontaneous warmth of greeting her tenseness was obvious, and she took refuge, as usual, in formality.

'Won't you come into the living-room?' she said. 'Mother will be right down.'

The living-room seemed, at first glance, conventional enough. The wallpaper was patterned in rose, and the mahogany furniture was simple. There were several overstuffed chairs, a couch with a green slip cover, and the usual number of small tables. But there were differences, too.

The mantelpiece had no ornament except a strange, almost terrifying object of twisted green china, with no particular shape, and holes at irrelevant intervals. The pictures on the walls were swirls of line and colour, featuring unaccompanied arms or legs or eyes – except for one simple sketch of a dancer which startled and impressed Sue, for the plainly visible signature read 'Picasso'.

Johnny stood in horrified fascination, staring at the object on the mantelpiece.

'What *is* it?' he breathed.

Cal grinned. 'It's an abstract ceramic,' she said. 'It's supposed to be "Man's Struggle", or something, but I think it looks like green fried eggs with the yolks out.'

'It's *awful*!' Johnny said.

'I think so too, but Mother likes it – goodness knows why.'

'Thank you for coming, Mrs Barry,' said a gruff voice, and Cal stiffened, looking at once apprehensive and uncertain as her mother entered the room.

Sue shook hands with Mrs Stuart. 'It was nice of you to ask us,' she said. 'You know Tabitha, of course, and these are my sons, Johnny and Jerry.'

'Hello,' said the twins in amiable chorus.

'Hello,' said Mona Stuart.

There was a pause in which she seemed to be struggling to recall the social rites she had abandoned for so long. Then the next step came to her. 'Sit down, won't you? Cornelia will bring us tea in a minute.'

Cornelia materialized almost at once with an elaborate tea tray. She smiled in acknowledgment of Sue's greeting.

A separate table had been arranged for Tabs and the twins, and Cal settled them around it with her usual ease where children were concerned.

Sue hoped that Mrs Stuart would notice this and say something complimentary to Cal. Unfortunately Mrs Stuart didn't, and Cal finally sat down beside Sue on the couch.

'Cal has been a real lifesaver to me this summer,' Sue said. 'She really has a knack with children, you know. They're always good with her.'

Mona Stuart glanced up, caught Sue's eye, and looked like a child caught reading a fairy story behind her geography book. 'That's fine! That's fine!' she responded hurriedly. 'Glad she's been a help. Er – I understand you've been teaching her something about nursing.'

'Oh, yes! She's learned a lot. In fact she's very good at it.'

'Well, well!' said Mona Stuart, with desperate facetiousness. 'Congratulations, Cal. I suppose you can set a leg with your eyes shut.'

Sue moaned inwardly, and Cal squirmed. 'Oh, *Mother*!' she protested. 'It isn't like that at all!'

Sue came to the rescue, speaking in generalities of the values of home nursing and of its limitations.

'Anyway,' Sue said, running down at last, 'Cal knows about bandaging and splints and strapping sprains and tourniquets and –'

'Tourniquet?' asked Mrs Stuart. 'I've heard that word before? What does it mean?'

Cal flushed. 'It's something you do to stop bleeding,' she said. 'You *must* know what it is, Mother. *Everybody* does.'

'Well, I didn't,' said Mona Stuart, 'but I'm glad you're learning useful things,' she added, with an awkward attempt at special interest. 'Perhaps you could show me how to work one.'

'You wouldn't care about it a bit, Mother,' Cal said, flatly.

The rebuff was so open that Sue felt a pang of sympathy for Mrs Stuart, who was, after all, doing her best. It was too bad of Cal to be so difficult, Sue thought, tactfully changing the subject to the commonplace one of the recent heat wave and the various means of escaping it.

'I took the children to the lake,' she said, 'as often as I could. Have you been out?'

'No,' said Mrs Stuart. 'I don't swim, so it doesn't seem worth it. But Cal said it was lovely. You swim pretty well, don't you, Cal?'

Cal looked startled. Then she flushed. 'Why – why yes, Mother.'

Tabitha looked up from her cambric tea and gingerbread.

'Cal's a *wonderful* swimmer,' Tabitha said. 'She's got a silver cup from her camp.'

'Oh, of course,' said Mrs Stuart hastily. 'I remember, now.'

'*I* can swim,' Tabitha said, 'only not the right way yet. The boys can't swim at all. Jerry jumped off the dock and he went right down to the bottom like a stone. Daddy had to jump in and fish him out.'

'He did not have to,' Jerry put in indignantly. 'I could have got myself out. I –'

Sue was not listening. If, during the discussion of the nursing lessons, she had sided with Cal's mother, it was now equally apparent why Cal behaved as she did. Mona Stuart might love her child. She might be trying to do the very best she could for her. The fact remained that Cal's fundamental reason for withdrawing from her mother remained valid. No matter how hard Mrs Stuart tried, she would not succeed, because she was not truly aware of Cal as a personality.

Jerry brought up the subject of the Bonneys, and this was also unfortunate.

'Dexter Bonney swam me out to the float,' he said. 'And d'you know what? He dived – *backwards*!'

'Bonney?' Mona Stuart inquired. 'Weren't those the children we met in the village, Cal? The ones who waved at you?'

'Oh, yes,' Cal said, indifferently, her eyes focused on the green ceramic. 'I – they were at Mrs Barry's picnic.'

'And they've got the darlingest baby,' Tabitha said. 'She's just beginning to crawl, and yesterday she crawled out on the lawn and ate *four* nasturtiums.'

'Was she sick?' Mrs Stuart asked with real interest.

It was extraordinary, Sue reflected, how much easier it was for this curious woman to talk to Tabitha than to her own child.

Aloud, Sue said, 'Probably not. When Tabitha was seven months old she crawled out on the back porch and ate the dog's dinner. I was petrified, but Bill only laughed. He said if it wouldn't hurt Maxl it wouldn't hurt the baby.'

Everybody was amused and the tension eased.

Then Mona Stuart said, casually, 'I was always terrified that Cal would get into my paints.'

It was an innocuous statement, but Sue watched the

cynical tightening of Cal's lips, and knew that Cal was telling herself that the fate of the expensive paints was what had most concerned her mother.

All in all, Sue decided when she got home, it had been a trying tea-party.

'East, west, home's best,' she said to Bill. 'I've helped them all I can, and a lot of good it's done! Next time remind me to stay at home and edge the dish towels with tatting.'

'What next time?' Bill asked with kindly interest. 'The next time someone asks you to tea? The next time someone's neurotic? The next time someone paints pictures? The next –'

'The next time someone interferes with my peace of mind. Or yours. Or the children's. The rest of this summer is going to be quiet and happy.'

It was – until the following week, when Johnny fell in love.

13

The toy-tree

JERRY's piano came and was established in the nursery – with the distinct understanding that it was not to be played at naptime, bedtime, or in the middle of the night. Sue had taken Jerry twice more to Miss Hallett's for brief instruction before the piano arrived, and in the interim was amazed and delighted by the change in him. He still hummed incessantly, or sat listening to the piano recordings Miss Hallett had given him, but his tantrums and restlessness had disappeared.

The piano had scarcely been rolled into place against the nursery wall before he settled himself before it, and with what appeared to Sue to be incredible dexterity, began to pick out simple tunes, accompanying himself in the bass with two-note chords, because, as he explained to Sue, his middle finger wouldn't go down very well – yet. He worked on this; he worked on scales; he tried out chords and harmonizing of his own until, daily, Sue had to insist on his stopping, to go out-of-doors and play.

Sue and Bill listened to him at the piano with astonishment, amusement, and pride. Veazie Ann, round-eyed, could only repeat, 'Stars alive!' Tabitha and Johnny, of course, tried out the piano, made hideous noises on it, and presently lost interest.

Johnny, however, was lonely when Jerry was practising and Sue was more than grateful to Cal, who exerted herself to amuse him. She helped him with whatever he was building; she took him for long walks with Tabitha and Maxl; she showed him how to dam the little brook in the pasture; she told him stories, many of which, aside from their basic idea, seemed to be her own inventions.

Sue had heard nothing further from Mrs Stuart. Cal never mentioned the tea-party and spoke of her mother only casually, but she didn't want to go anywhere, even with Sue – a fact which became evident the day that Johnny fell in love.

Sue was driving down to the village and, as usual, intended to take any or all of the children. Jerry was practising and as Sue paused in the nursery door he was playing an odd little melody which she had never heard before.

'That's pretty, darling,' she said. 'What is it? Do you want to go to the village?'

'It isn't anything, Mummy,' Jerry said without turning. 'I just heard it in my head. I'd rather stay here. Will you bring me a popsicle?'

Sue promised and went on, unaware that her son had just composed his first piece of music. She found Cal and Johnny lying in the shade on the side lawn, watching Tabitha make a hollyhock doll. As Sue came across the grass Cal was saying:

'So Jimmie went away crying, because they had forgotten him and he was the only child at the Prince's party who didn't get a present. It was a long way home and the more he cried the worse he felt, and then, all of a sudden, he saw it!' Cal paused.

'Saw what?' Johnny demanded, squirming. 'Go on, Cal! What was it?'

'It was a little tree, no taller than you are, but it had all kinds of toys growing on it, and balloons, and candy, and oranges, and all *sorts* of things. There was a little sign on it, and Jimmie read it, and it said, "Give me a good home and take care of me and I will reward you." So Jimmie dug it up very carefully, and carried it home and planted it, and guess what?'

'I know!' Johnny shouted. 'He picked all the toys!'

'Oh, better than that – it grew and grew, and it was *always* covered with toys – different ones at different times – and more and more – and they were all for Jimmie, as many as he could possibly want, for ever and ever! So Jimmie didn't feel badly about the Prince's party any more.'

Johnny sighed rapturously. 'Oooo!' he said. He sat up abruptly. 'Cal! Do you think we could find a toy-tree?'

'Of course not,' said Tabitha with a big-sisterly scorn. 'It's only a story – but a wonderful story, Cal.'

'It certainly is,' said Sue, who had come up unnoticed. 'Anybody want to go to the village?'

Tabitha and Johnny did, but Cal shook her head. 'No, thank you,' she said. 'I don't care if I never go to the village.'

'Goodness, Cal,' said Sue laughing. 'Why not?'

'Oh, I don't know,' said Cal fretfully. 'I'd just rather be here.'

'All right, my dear,' said Sue, giving up.

They left her there, staring dreamily up at the cream-puff August clouds drifting across the sky.

Sue had a long grocery list and the children would be hot, waiting in the car, so she took them into the store with her, gave them ice cream cones, and turned her attention to the marketing. She never had to worry about the children, in stores, even when they were much smaller, for they were obedient about not touching anything, and tried earnestly to keep out from under the grown-ups' feet.

Sue's order had been filled except for the meat when she heard somebody say, 'Land sakes! Look at that! Ain't that cute?' She turned quickly. Tabitha was gazing with appetite at the pictures on boxes of fancy cookies, but Johnny's red head was at the other side of the store, beside the candy counter. With him was a little girl in a pink dress, probably about his age, but she was tiny and delicate looking with great blue eyes. A tangle of pale golden curls made a fuzz all over her head. She was patting Johnny's cheek, her face serious and admiring. 'You're *nice*,' she stated clearly.

There was sudden quiet in the store as the surprised and delighted Johnny stammered, 'I – you're – I like *you*!'

They gazed at one another in innocent happiness, and no one in the store laughed.

'I'm Anne,' the little girl said. 'What's your name?'

'Johnny.'

'Will you come and play at my house, Johnny?'

'Yes, I will!' said Johnny with fervour, and then, being Johnny, sensibly inquired. 'Where is it?'

'I'll have to ask Mummy.' She looked over her shoulder and called, 'Mummy, where is our house?'

'Montgomery Road,' said a voice behind Sue – who swung around to encounter the amused and friendly eyes of a young woman in the shorts-and-shirt garb of the summer vacationist.

Sue smiled at her. 'May my son call on your daughter? We live on Montgomery Road, too.'

'Oh, is that your little boy? It would be wonderful if he could come. Anne's been so lonely with no other children to play with, and we'll be here another week. We've rented one of the Bald Trail Inn cottages. Oh, and I'm Leila Murray.'

'I'm Sue Barry. We live in that white house just after the last turn up.'

'Oh, yes.'

They shook hands, agreeing to make arrangements about the children by telephone the next morning, but when they tried to separate Anne and Johnny, to go home, they ran into difficulties.

Anne burst into tears, and Johnny – steady, sensible Johnny – cried desperately, 'No! No!'

They were finally persuaded to part, their mothers promising that Johnny should play at Anne's house in the morning, and that Anne would visit Johnny's house in the afternoon, after her nap.

Sue told Bill about it that night when the children were in bed. 'It was dear, Bill. Johnny talked about her all the way home – though I suppose by tomorrow afternoon they'll be hitting each other over the head.'

'Not necessarily,' said Bill. 'It's not uncommon for kids that age to fall pretty seriously in love, for a short while. After all, it's their first realization that they can find responsive affection outside their immediate families, and while it lasts it hits them plenty hard.'

'What does one do – leave it alone?'

'Sure. What else?'

Sue left it alone as best she could, in view of the fact that either she or Mrs Murray must transport the children daily from one house to the other.

' "Neither snow, nor rain, nor heat, nor gloom of night" are going to keep Johnny from his beloved,' said Sue to Bill after three days of this. 'They go around hand in hand, or with their arms around each other, and if you could see Johnny helping that little thing up steps and over rocks! I'd no idea he could be so gallant.'

'Why not? Look at his father!'

'I am,' said Sue. 'That's what surprises me! Johnny's given her all his toys, too – though fortunately she's not addicted to saws and hammers and forgets to take them home. Poor Jerry's nose is dreadfully out of joint, and Tabitha has gone all maternal and treats her like a kind of superdoll.'

It was on the afternoon of the Murrays' last day at the Inn that Mrs Murray, faithfully bringing Anne over for the afternoon, decided, on Sue's urging, to stay herself.

'I don't suppose I ought,' she said, taking the porch chair Sue pulled forward, 'but I'm just about packed, and Al has gone off for a final orgy of fishing; he won't be home until all hours. Goodness, I don't see how Anne can tell the twins apart, but she does – every time.'

'The eye of love,' said Sue. 'Look at them.'

The children were all playing in the sand pile, Anne sitting close to Johnny. Jerry was ignoring her, and Tabitha was hovering over her tenderly when Johnny rose suddenly, took Anne by the hand, and stalked towards the house.

'Mummy,' he said through the screen door, his freckles standing out with shock. 'Anne says she's going away tomorrow. She isn't, is she? *Is* she?'

'I'm afraid she must, darling,' Sue told him. 'Her father and mother have to go back to the city. Their vacation is over. I told you about it, Johnny.' She had indeed tried to prepare him, but the words had meant little then. Now reality was upon him.

'Why can't she live here with us, and be your little girl?'

'Because she'd be unhappy without her own mother.'

'Well, I'm here,' said Johnny simply.

'I'm sorry, Johnny,' said Sue. 'She must.'

He turned without a word, his face quivering, and

dashed around the corner of the house, out of sight. Anne, infinitesimal in her yellow sun suit, ran after him. 'Johnny! Johnny!' she called, and began to cry as she ran.

The two mothers looked at each other, their throats aching. Leila Murray's eyes were wet.

'What'll we *do*?' she asked. 'Ought we to go after them?'

Sue shook her head, swallowed, and said carefully, 'No. I – it might be better to let them alone.'

It was perhaps ten minutes later that Leila Murray caught sight of them, clambering hand-in-hand up the hill pasture.

'Johnny!' Sue shouted. 'Come back! Just for a minute!'

The children turned slowly and trudged back.

'What is it, Mummy?' Johnny asked at the porch door. He was looking much more cheerful and so was Anne.

'Darling,' said Sue gently, 'Anne's too little to be dragged way up there. She isn't used to woods and hills. Couldn't you play here?'

'We weren't playing. I was going to find a toy-tree for Anne, and she can take it home and have lots of presents, and they'll *all* be from me – all the time.'

'Oh, Johnny!' said Sue involuntarily. This was really heartbreaking. 'There isn't a toy-tree up the hill. It was a fairy story, dear. You know that.'

Johnny shook his head, suddenly stubborn, and after a moment Sue understood. With part of his mind he knew that the toy-tree wasn't real, but the desire to do something wonderful for Anne, the need for a great gesture, eased his distress and demanded belief. Failing to find the toy-tree would be less important than the fact that he had done his utmost.

'One might have come there last night,' Johnny said. 'I want to look.'

'Where is it that he wants to go?' Leila Murray asked.

'To the upper end of that hill pasture. There's a big strip of birch grove up there, where the children play a good deal. It's not that it isn't all right – they always stay in the grove, and it's within yelling distance of the house – but it's quite a climb for Anne, when she's not used to it, and –'

'Oh, let them go – it won't hurt Anne. Probably do her good.'

'Well,' said Sue. Then, 'If she's going up there we'd better put her into a pair of Johnny's overalls and a jersey. She'll be scratched to pieces in that sun suit.'

The children set off at last, liberally doused with mosquito repellant and carrying the usual bag of biscuits and peanut butter sandwiches. Anne looked very tiny and ridiculously feminine in Johnny's too large overalls.

Sue and Leila Murray watched the small figures growing smaller among the hillside boulders until they disappeared among the birches.

'If I could have foreseen this,' said Sue, returning to her porch chair, 'I'd have had a toy-tree ready for them up there – balloons and all.' She sighed. 'The poor babies. Isn't all this emotion getting you down? How about some refreshments?'

'I'd love some.' Mrs Murray sat for a moment, thinking. Then she said, 'You know, Al has always come up here in the hunting season, and this time I believe I'll come with him. It must be perfectly beautiful – and it would give the kids something to look forward to. I can't bear them to feel that this is a for-ever-and-ever parting.'

They discussed this over sandwiches and tea, watching Tabitha and Jerry at work in the sand pile; Tabitha systematic, Jerry bursting with energy. Then the talk drifted into a consideration of the problems of bringing

up children in general and their own in particular. Leila
Murray, Sue discovered, had an immense fund of common
sense. She was in no way intellectual, her education had
been average and didn't seem to have 'taken', but she
had warmth, kindness, and a down-to-earth wisdom
which Sue found very refreshing.

The conversation, Sue reflected as they talked, was
unquestionably of the type which is lampooned in novels
and jeered at by the unthinking, yet it dealt with matters
which had been fundamental and highly important since
the beginning of time. Without children, Sue and Leila
Murray would have had nothing in common. As it was,
they shared a rich world of experiences, interests, and hopes.

It was some time later that Jerry interrupted them. He
and Tabitha had been so engrossed in their elaborate
sand castle that they hadn't noticed the departure of
Johnny and Anne, but now Jerry began to miss his twin
and came to the porch to demand, simultaneously
Johnny, a drink of water, and a dill pickle.

Mrs Murray glanced at her watch. 'Heavens!' she said.
'It's quarter to five! We'd better get the children down.
It's going to be a long drive tomorrow and I want Anne
to have an early supper and go to bed.'

Sue was, herself, a little startled at the lateness of the
hour, and rose at once to bring a huge, old-fashioned
dinner bell from the kitchen.

'This always means come-at-once,' she said, laughing,
and rang it lustily from the back door.

There was no answering whoop from the hillside, and
no sign of any small, overalled figures among the birches.
She waited a minute or two and then rang again. There
was still no response and she began to lose patience.

'Love,' she said grimly, 'is one thing – but making me
climb that hill is another.'

Mrs Murray glanced at her. 'There isn't anything they could get into up there – is there?'

'Absolutely not. No roads, no cars, no water except small springs and tiny brooks, no caves, no holes – and the children never go beyond the birches. All we have to worry about is the character of a young man who doesn't bring his girl home when his mother calls him.'

She rang the bell once more, with no result.

'All right for you, Sonny,' she said to the absent Johnny. Then, to Mrs Murray, 'If you'll excuse me I'll just run up and get them. No, Jerry, you stay here with Tabs. Mrs Murray has to go home right away, and I can go up that hill a lot faster without you. Run along and play, darling. I'll be right back.'

'I believe I'll come with you,' said Mrs Murray suddenly.

They left the disgruntled Jerry pouting after them and, cutting across the vegetable garden, began the steep climb up the hill. Sue was accustomed to it, but Mrs Murray was panting when they reached the grove, and she sat down on the nearest rock.

'*Johnny! Anne!*' Sue called, and waited.

The only sound was the chattering of birch leaves in the breeze, and for the first time Sue felt the cold clutch of terror. It was silly, she knew, and she fought it back as best she could. Suppose they *had* gone a little way into the deep woods beyond the grove – they couldn't have gone far. She could easily find them.

Leila Murray was no longer sitting on the rock. She was standing, her face a little pale.

'They might have dropped asleep,' she said quietly. 'If they did they probably wouldn't hear us. Anne sleeps like the – Anne sleeps very soundly.'

'So does Johnny.' But Sue didn't think Johnny had fallen asleep – though if Anne had he might be just sitting there beside her. Her mind fastened upon this thought, holding back the blind, unreasoning panic which was tightening her throat and pounding against her ribs.

Elderberry bushes, sweet fern, and sumac prevented her from seeing the ground for any distance in one direction, and granite boulders and huckleberry bushes effectively screened the other. Some of those boulders were high, and Johnny, like any other child, loved to climb. Suppose Anne, exhausted by all this unusual activity, *had* dropped asleep, and Johnny, bored, had scrambled up one of those gigantic monsters? Suppose he had slipped or lost his balance?

She saw him lying there.

'We'd better start searching the grove,' she said, and wondered that her numb lips could form the words. 'We'll start in the middle. You work towards one end, and I'll work towards the other. And keep yelling. It'll wake them in case we happen to miss seeing them.'

They tramped back and forth, shouting in the sun-dappled woods, and their voices echoed back, thin and small and childlike, from some unseen flank of the mountain.

'Johnny! Anne!' the faint echoes called cruelly, each time bringing the hearts of the two mothers into their throats.

The children were not in the grove, nor was there any mark to show which way they might have gone. The dry ground was like iron, yielding no small footprints. There were broken branches and newly trampled sweet fern in the grove, but beyond it, among the pines, there was nothing except an occasional scuffed place in the pine needles. Anything – any woods creature – could have scuffed up the needles.

Sue and Leila went as far into the pine woods as they

could without getting lost. They kept close together, now, their voices hoarse from shouting. They avoided one another's eyes. Sue's heartbeats crashed in her chest, her mouth was dry, and the pit of her stomach was a hard, icy knot, its coldness spreading over her entire body. She and Leila talked when they were not shouting. They talked steadily, they talked sensibly, trying to drive from the screen of dark horror in their minds the bright and dreadful pictures they saw there.

'This is stupid,' said Sue at last. 'We're only wasting time. They can't have gone far, but they might have gone up the mountain, or around it and down. We'd better go home and get help.'

'Whatever you say.' Leila turned, and without warning broke into a stumbling run, her eyes suddenly glassy.

Sue caught her by the arm, fighting down her own panic. 'No!' she said sharply. 'Walk! You've got to! You'll collapse before we're half-way back if you don't. Save your strength.'

Leila stared at her wildly and Sue's grip tightened painfully on her arm.

'Thank you,' said Leila after a moment. 'I'll be all right now.'

Sue never knew what route they took home, nor how long it was before she felt the familiar smoothness of the porch doorknob under her hand and heard her own voice speaking briefly to Veazie Ann, to Bill, on the telephone, and then saying clearly, 'Operator? The State police, please!'

14

'Not very far'

BILL and the State trooper reached the house within five minutes of each other – Bill first.

Sue ran to meet him, clinging to him in wordless anguish. He held her close, trying almost by main force, to protect her from her own pain, though his face was as white as hers.

'It'll be all right,' he was saying when the motor-cycle roared up the lane.

The State trooper was big, kind, and very competent, and Sue, with Bill's steadying arm around her, tried to answer all the questions exactly. Leila Murray, who had come out when she heard the motor-cycle, stood quietly in the lane beside Sue. Her face was flushed and her eyes were too bright, and she held Anne's little yellow sun suit, turning it over and over in her hands.

She had tried to reach her husband at the Inn, but he had not yet returned, so she had left a message, explaining, telling him to call her at Sue's, or come there at once. So far there had been no word from him, and she seemed to Sue to be dreadfully alone, standing there.

The State trooper snapped shut the notebook in which he had written the facts as Sue gave them to him.

'Now don't you worry,' he said. 'We'll find them all right. Little kids like that never get very far. May I use your telephone, Doctor?'

He seemed so sure, and when he and Bill had gone

into the house, Leila and Sue, following more slowly,
looked at one another with brighter faces. If they
could have known that the children were unhurt – they
avoided any other word – they would have been almost
cheerful.

But they didn't know and the hideous pictures in their
minds continued to repeat themselves. So they talked,
but once inside the house neither could sit down for
long. They wandered from room to room, always finding
themselves, in the end, somewhere near Veazie Ann,
whose calmness and certainty that everything would be
all right helped both mothers – though it didn't deceive
them.

'Land,' Veazie Ann said, 'them State police is wonderful. And they got near an hour before sundown, too, and
a-plenty of light after that. It'll be an awful warm night,
too, and not a cloud in the sky. Them kids'll just curl up
like bunnies and go to sleep – and wake up in their own
beds. They're dressed good to be out, too, and they had
a mess of sandwiches and biscuits. They won't hardly
know anything's happened.'

'But they'll be so thirsty!' Leila said desperately.

'Thirsty nothin'! There's springs all over everywhere,
and Johnny knows how to drink from 'em. He'll show
Anne.'

It was Veazie Ann who had suggested sending Jerry
and Tabitha to the Todds' to spend the night, and Sue
had agreed reluctantly. She wanted the children where
she could look at them and touch them, but she knew it
would be better for them to be out of the excitement and
away from her own anguish of mind. They wouldn't
sleep, anyway, with cars and motor-cycles and people
coming and going.

Sue had had to explain to them a little of what had

happened, since they had been having their supper on the porch when she returned without Johnny.

'Johnny and Anne,' she had told them, 'went so far into the woods I guess they couldn't find the way home, but it's all right. Daddy will find them.'

The children accepted this, but they would not have done so for long, and sending them to the Todds' was the only solution. Besides, spending the night at Aunt Martha's was always a special treat for them.

It was Veazie Ann who gave them their baths while the State trooper was questioning Sue. It was Veazie Ann who kept them busy upstairs until the Todds' car came for them, and the smiling Sue put them into it with a desperately cheerful hug and a kiss apiece.

They left not a moment too soon. The Todds' car had scarcely disappeared before a State police truck and police cars filled with troopers began to arrive. The lane swarmed with uniformed men. The truck was filled with ropes, axes, floodlights, first-aid equipment of all kinds, food and hot coffee for the troopers, and a radio sending-and-receiving set. A man would remain on duty in the truck to operate the radio.

Sue had put a comforting arm around Leila, and they stood on the back steps, watching with mounting hope.

'Lord love a duck!' said Veazie Ann behind them. 'They could find a penny in the North Woods with such a business as that!'

Leila nodded agreement, but Sue wished they'd hurry. Sue hadn't told Leila that there were bears and wild cats in the mountains – to say nothing of snakes. What were they waiting for, anyway? They seemed to be all organized in groups and ready to start.

She learned what they were waiting for a few minutes later, just as the last rays of precious sunlight vanished.

A police car, coming at high speed, swung abruptly into the lane and parked behind the last car. The door opened, and a State trooper got out. With him, straining and slavering on leashes, were two immense bloodhounds with dangling ears and flopping jowls.

Sue gasped, and Leila made a faint sound, half sob, half moan.

My baby! Sue thought wildly. Yet after the first shock she was glad and relieved. Now the children would certainly be found and without waste of time and effort.

'Sue!' Bill called. 'Bring out some of the children's clothing – quickly, dear! The dogs have to have it to get the scent.'

Leila was still clutching Anne's sun suit, and hurried forward with it. Sue dashed into the house for Johnny's coat. The officers took both and did not return them.

Five minutes later the lane was empty of state troopers, and promptly began to fill with other men and boys – friends, neighbours, strangers, a boy scout or two in uniform, with word of more to come.

'I – let's go in,' Leila said. 'When I think about all this being for – for –'

They went in – and stood around the living-room. Sue heard the back door slam, and Cal's voice, shrill with excitement and distress.

'Oh, Veazie Ann! I heard on the radio! How awful! Poor Mrs Barry, and the other lady! What *made* Johnny go off like that?'

'He had a notion to find a toy-tree – though 'twarn't like him to go straggling off into the deep woods after it.'

'Toy-tr – but I – then it's *my* fault! I told him about –' Her voice broke. 'Where's Mrs Barry? I've *got* to see her!'

'Cal,' said Veazie Ann quietly, 'you'll do no such a

thing! Sue's in no state to listen to you talk nonsense – for 'tis nonsense, and you know it. You go right straight along home and be sensible. Scoot along now! There isn't a thing to do here but wait.'

There was a moment of silence. Then the door slammed and Cal ran down the steps. Poor Cal. But Sue was relieved that Veazie Ann had done the managing. Enough was enough.

The telephone was beginning to ring, now. Veazie Ann took charge of it.

Sue felt numb. The icy knot of fear was still in the pit of her stomach but she was too tired to be conscious of it, or of its effect on her. Johnny! Johnny! The word beat steadily in her brain with the beating of her heart. She sat down heavily on the living-room couch and sprang to her feet instantly, hearing a shout outside. It was only a new group of searchers arriving.

Leila, too, was wearing out with the strain. Her feverish colour was gone and her eyes looked dull. Sue wished her husband would come – but when he did, at last, a huge, bull-necked man, he was white and shaking and it was Leila who did the supporting, the calming, the encouraging.

Once he looked over at Sue. 'Well, *you've* got two others,' he said.

'Al!' Leila almost screamed.

'Sorry,' Al mumbled.

The hours dragged by, each minute a long-drawn tensity of waiting, of listening, of straining for every sound. Towards midnight Sue went outside and talked for a time with the radio operator in the police truck, asking him about his work, about police methods – anything. She was still there when she heard heavy footsteps on the hillside and a sound of panting and snuffling. A moment later three shadowy figures stepped out of the night into the glare of the floodlights on the truck.

The dogs had come back.

'*What is it! What's happened!*' Sue's voice was scarcely more than a whisper.

The trooper wiped his forehead with the back of his sleeve. 'They lost the scent,' he said wearily.

Sue felt as if every drop of blood had been drained from her entire body. But she mustn't faint; she *must* know.

'Why?' she managed to say.

'Well, m'am, the children kind of spiraled down one side of the mountain and there was a marshy place – oh no, nothing to hurt – only a couple of inches deep – but the Forestry Department had sprayed it over with DDT. If I'd known, I wouldn't have taken the dogs too near. It injures their noses so they can't smell. I'm sorry, Mrs Barry. But that doesn't mean we won't find the kids pretty soon – give you my word. We came on the paper bag where they had their sandwiches – close by a spring. Looks like you've got a pretty smart little boy.'

'Thank you, Officer. Thank you very much.'

'Not much to thank me for. But the Doctor said to tell you to hold on – he'd be back soon, and don't worry.'

Sue nodded, unable to speak, and moved away into the faint moonlight. She wished she could cry – really cry – bawl – howl – not just choke to death. Dear Bill! Darling Bill! But she'd better go in and tell the others. At least Leila could know the children weren't hungry or thirsty.

It was around three o'clock that Sue fell asleep in one of the porch chairs. It was a fitful, nightmarish sleep, but it was rest of a sort, and when she woke she saw that daylight was coming over the mountains in a thin wash of pale gold. Nothing else was changed. The police cars

and truck were there, but the floodlight had been turned
off. One or two men had come in. Sue looked over her
shoulder, through the kitchen window into the living-
room, and saw that Al was asleep on the couch, his head
in Leila's lap. Leila was not asleep – nor was Veazie Ann,
rocking quietly in the kitchen. As Sue looked, Veazie
Ann got up and reached out to put out the kitchen light,
which was no longer necessary. Her hand paused, half-
way.

Sue, too, was immobile, her ears straining.

The next moment Veazie Ann was on the porch. 'Sue!
Sue! The bell! They're found!'

'What bell?' said Sue idiotically.

'The big dinner bell – hear it? Bill took it with him to
let us know!'

'*Leila!*' Sue shrieked. '*Leila, they're found!*'

But she couldn't wait for Leila, nor for Veazie Ann.
She was out, racing along the lane past the barn, and
down, the bell clanging louder as she ran, until at last
she saw a boy scout – Dexter Bonney – a swift, khaki-
coloured figure sprinting towards her in the pale morning
light, and ringing the bell furiously. He was grinning
almost literally from ear to ear.

'Deck!' Sue gasped. 'Are they all right?'

'Sure, Coming right along behind me.'

It was a long procession which came up over the hill –
a procession led by Bill with Johnny in his arms. Behind
him came the State trooper who had questioned Sue. A
small golden head rested drowsily on his broad shoulder.
Behind him, in ones and twos were some twenty State
troopers, a sprinkling of very tired boy scouts trudging
in the rear.

Johnny's voice came up to Sue on the morning breeze.
'Mummy! Mummy!' and in another minute he was in

her arms, whole, breathing. His face was streaked with dirt, tears, and berry stains, but he was smiling.

Sue and Bill looked at each other over his dirty, tousled red head, a long look, indescribable.

Anne lifted her curls from the trooper's shoulder, saw her mother and father running as they had never run before, and held out her soft small arms. 'I got my feet wet, Mummy,' she said.

15

All over

THE children were far more exhausted than they had first seemed in their excitement and Leila decided to stay over another day and return to the city by train. Al would go on as planned with their car.

'Thank you a lot,' she said to Bill and Sue, who offered her the guest room, 'but I think Anne will be quieter at the cottage. If we stay here it's going to be impossible to keep her in bed.'

Bill applied soothing lotions to the children's gnat and mosquito bites, which were not too severe – thanks to the insect repellant which Sue had put on. It had, of course, lost much of its effectiveness in a few hours, but it had helped, and the Murrays, after hearing the pieced-together account of the search, and Johnny's story, took the heavily sleeping Anne back to the Inn.

Johnny was put to bed as soon as they had gone, for though he insisted that he wasn't tired, his freckles looked enormous; there were dark, purple circles under his eyes, and his lids drooped in spite of his effort to keep them up.

Sue rocked him to sleep, holding him close against her while she thought about the long night.

Johnny's story, naturally, had been sketchy. A four-year-old notices only what impresses himself, not what seems important to grown-ups, but he was clear enough about how they had become lost. They had gone back into the grove looking eagerly for the toy-tree, certain that they would come upon it at any moment, and were scampering along near the edge of the pines when Anne gave a scream of excitement.

'There it is, Johnny! Look! See the candle?' And she had started off, straight into the deep woods.

What she had actually seen, no one knew, but Bill thought that it must have been a flash of sunlight on the mica in a granite rock. The toy-tree, vague in her mind, was associated with Christmas, and she had been prepared for glitter.

Johnny, strictly forbidden to leave the birch grove, had run back and forth calling to her to come back. Then, as she ran deeper into the woods, he succumbed to his urge to find the toy-tree and ran after her. The flash of light, had, of course, vanished at once, but both children were now convinced that the toy-tree really was close at hand and everything else was forgotten, including time, rules, and direction.

'We couldn't find the tree,' said Johnny sadly, 'and Anne started to cry and wanted to go home, but I couldn't find the grove, either. I guess I went the wrong way. I'll never go in those awful woods again, Mummy.'

The shoulder of the mountain was level for some distance beyond the birches, and then rose steeply up, to the south, but to the southwest it sloped gradually downward into miles of densely wooded valleys and hills.

Home had been due north.

'All the same,' Bill said, 'habit, or some vague instinct, must have been what started him *down*. He isn't old enough to figure it out – but he always has gone down to get home. The dogs traced them in spirals. The kids circled as people do when they're lost like that, but every time the circling started to take them up they turned and went the other way – down.'

The shallow marshy spot where the dogs had lost the trail had been scarcely visible because of the thick grass growing in it and the children had splashed through it, both crying by this time. They had not gone far beyond the marsh for they had come upon a tumble of rocks still warm from the sun. They had crawled into a crevice, instinctively seeking shelter, and grateful for the warmth. There they had cuddled down, close together, and cried themselves to sleep.

Bill's searching party had found them just at dawn. The men had been over the ground several times, but the children were too deeply asleep to hear them, and were invisible in their niche. It was not until Johnny crawled out at daybreak, and stood up, that one of the troopers caught sight of his bright blue jersey.

Well, it was all over now.

Sue rose at last and tucked her safely sleeping son into his bed. Then she went downstairs. Her bones still felt as if they were made of solid iron and her mind refused to function.

Bill, on his way to a hot soaking bath, met her at the foot of the stairs and glanced at her sharply. 'You'd better go to bed yourself,' he said.

'Maybe I will, after a while, but I can't seem to settle, even in a bed, right now.'

She went on out to the kitchen where Veazie Ann was washing Bill's breakfast dishes.

'How about some toast and coffee, Sue – and maybe a soft-boiled egg? You ain't eat a thing since Johnny got lost.'

Sue nodded, and wandered over to the window to look out. It was nearly eight o'clock now, but some of the neighbours were still returning from the search. 'Poor things,' Sue murmured. 'They've been so kind. I wish we could let them know.'

'It's too bad, but ye can't help it if folks go off all harum-scarum without taking thought. Did you know that Cal didn't go home last night?'

'*What?*'

'No, she didn't. Deck Bonney told me. Seems she went out from here and seen the boy scouts a-gathering, and darned if she didn't make 'em take her along – on account of she knows so much about first-aid. I telephoned her mother about an hour ago, so she wouldn't worry. She didn't know Cal was gone. Fact, she didn't even know Cal come over here last night. She said Cal went upstairs awful early and was a-listening to the radio, and then her light went out. The tarnation young one must've skipped off without a word.'

'Well, she'd be all right with the boy scouts. I hope she's home by now.'

'Like enough. You want I should call up Martha and have her send Jerry and Tabs home? She'd love to keep 'em till after lunch – and you look all in, Sue.'

'I'm perfectly all right,' said Sue firmly, her hand shaking so that she spilled her coffee. 'They can come home whenever Martha wants to send them.'

Veazie Ann made no comment but privately decided to send for the children later. She put two soft-boiled eggs and toast on the kitchen table. 'Eat that, now,' she was saying, as she would have said it to a child, when she glanced up and saw Mona Stuart in the doorway.

'Good morning,' Mrs Stuart said. 'I'm sorry to intrude on you, Mrs Barry. You must be exhausted. But Cal isn't home yet and I thought – no, don't get up, please. Go on with your breakfast. I'm very happy to hear that

Johnny is all right.' She sat down in Veazie Ann's rocker.

'Cal's all right, too,' Veazie Ann assured her. 'All the boy scouts ain't back yet. Care for a cup of coffee?'

'Thank you, yes.'

Sue found her voice with some difficulty. This was not going to be her best day for dealing with people or situations.

'I'm sorry about Cal,' she said. 'The child rushed out with the idea that it was all her fault that Johnny got lost.'

Sue explained in more detail and Mona Stuart listened, her expression both distressed and exasperated.

'Well,' she snapped, when Sue had finished, 'she might, at least, have let me know.'

'Young ones,' said Veazie Ann, 'don't stop to think. They git upset and away they go. Like enough the boys was just starting off and wouldn't wait for her to call you. And she knew we wouldn't have let her go. You got to be patient with her, Mrs Stuart. Cal meant all right – and she's going to be awful tired.'

Mona Stuart's face softened. 'I know. I'll try.'

Sue had just finished her breakfast when the last group of boy scouts straggled down the hill pasture. Cal was with them.

Mrs Stuart rose and went to the porch door.

Cal dashed across the lawn, dirty and bedraggled but with a happy face. 'We heard!' she cried to the dimly seen figure through the screen. 'Oh, Mrs Barry, I'm so gl – why, *Mother*!'

'Cal,' Mrs Stuart said, her tone as kind as she could make it, 'why didn't you get word to me, some way? I wouldn't have kept you from going if I'd known how you felt.'

Cal was on the defensive at once. 'I know you wouldn't,' she said bitterly, 'but you wouldn't have known how I felt if I'd talked for forty years! You'd just have said I was silly.'

Sue didn't dare interfere, though she wanted to, for Cal, obviously worn out and overwrought, was in no condition to be reasonable. The danger signals were already apparent. Cal's face, which had been flushed, was now pale, and her lips trembled. One hand was tightly clenched in the palm of the other.

'I wouldn't have thought you were silly,' Mona Stuart unwisely persisted. 'I think I'd have understood – but even if I didn't you shouldn't have gone off like that. I didn't dream you were out of the house until Mrs Cooney telephoned me this morning. And then you didn't come back. I've been worried to death.'

The storm broke.

'*You've* been worried!' Cal sobbed. 'You didn't even know I was gone! You just said so yourself! *You – worried!* That's a scream! Look at Mrs Barry! She's the one who worried. I guess she's been half crazy all night, just because I told Johnny – I – *She* really *loves* her children!' And then, appalled at what she had said, Cal flung herself into a chair and buried her face in her arms.

Mona Stuart turned without a word, her face quivering, and went heavily through the kitchen into the living-room. Cal, whose sobs – howls, in fact – prevented her from hearing her mother's retreat, continued her hysterical crying.

Veazie Ann would have gone out on the porch at once, but Sue shook her head.

'I'll do it,' she told Veazie Ann, and pushed back her chair.

'Lordy mercy, Sue, you hadn't ought to have no more on you right now.'

'Never mind,' said Sue grimly. 'It may be just as well.'

She went out on the porch and stood for a moment looking at the sobbing figure huddled in the chair. It was easy, Sue realized, to be angry in her present state of nervous exhaustion, and she encouraged her anger – but not too much. She had no desire to lose her own self-control, and it was at the snapping point.

She took three steps across the porch and gripped Cal by the shoulder.

'Stop that yelping at once!'

Cal looked up, her swollen eyes widening at the expression on Sue's face.

'Cal Stuart, if you were my child I'd take you across my knee and blister you with the back of a hairbrush. No, I don't want to hear a word! You're a silly, self-centred little girl, so sorry for yourself that you can't see anything else.'

Cal stared in frozen silence, and Sue went on.

'Your mother is a good woman, and a fine woman, and she loves you dearly. She's been trying all summer to tell you so, and anybody less wrapped up in herself than you would have seen it. Everybody *else* knows it! You've frightened her to death with your silly, childish, self-important impulses, and you've just hurt her horribly.'

The shock in Cal's face had given place to incredulity.

'I – I've – hurt her?' she stammered. 'I couldn't. She doesn't love me that much!'

'She's in the other room – *crying*.'

'M-Mother's – crying? Oh, no!' Cal sprang out of her chair and hurled herself through the kitchen and into the living-room. 'Mother – darling!' Sue heard. 'Oh – *Mummy*!'

After a long interval Sue tiptoed to the living-room door and looked in.

Mona Stuart, in her stained white coat and with her

black hair straggling, was sitting in one of the big arm-chairs. On her lap she held the long-legged, beautiful, tear-streaked Cal – whose head was on her mother's shoulder. And Mona Stuart, the tough, the undemonstra-tive, was humming the Brahms 'Lullaby' while she awkwardly stroked Cal's dirty cheek.

She turned away, swallowed, and, flinging herself into Veazie Ann's arms, burst into tears at last.

'There now, my baby,' said Veazie Ann tenderly. 'That's *good.*'

16

Sue is not satisfied

SUE picked up the receiver and her 'hello' was answered by the voice of Miss Minnie Batson. Miss Batson, however, had a much more impressive way of announcing herself.

'*Winslow Gazette*, Society Department,' she said. 'Have you any news for us this week?'

Sue knew that Miss Batson was paid twenty-five cents per item for Springdale news, and that she needed the money.

Sue tried hard. 'Honestly, I don't think there's a thing,' she said. 'I'll be having some people in for dinner when we get the peaches put up, but this past week –'

Even over the telephone she could sense Miss Minnie's disappointment and as she glanced out through the open front door she was suddenly inspired.

'Wait a minute! I have quite a few people here, now, and I'm giving them tea. Would that do?'

'Just tell me who's there, that's all,' said Miss Minnie briskly.

Sue gave her the names and hung up, grinning. When the *Gazette* came out next Thursday there would be a little paragraph:

'Mrs William Barry, of Montgomery Road entertained at tea on Tuesday. Among those present were –'

It would all be true, but somehow the scene on the lawn

was lacking in the atmosphere of tranquil grace associated with afternoon tea.

Not that the setting wasn't perfect.

Everything swam in a dappling of August sunlight and heavy green shadow. An occasional medallion of bright yellow fluttered from the elms, but the maples stood in rich, full leaf, proudly untouched by any threat of approaching autumn. The flower borders were bright with marigolds and zinnias, and tall stalks of peach, gold, and scarlet gladiolas. The house was white and serene, its doors and windows hospitably open to the warm afternoon. On the lawn blue chairs were grouped around a white table laden with pitchers of milk and ice tea, and plates of cake and cookies.

There, however, the resemblance ceased. Instead of being a background for the gentle chiming of polite conversation, the house and garden seethed with unorganized bedlam.

Johnny and Jerry and the three middle Bonneys were engaged in a furious game of hide-and-seek, played with more enthusiasm than science. Its principal feature involved dashing across the lawn, screaming with excitement.

Cathy Bonney, now an independent eight months, was sitting in the middle of a clump of zinnias in a state of indescribable squalor. She was smearing a slimy zwiebach over her face and thoughtfully consuming a pink flower.

Tabitha was swinging and singing – the former very high; the latter very loud and off key:

> Free from WARDS – in Chancery –
> Up in the AIR – sky high, sky high

Her pigtails were flying and her little face was alight with the ecstasy of flight.

Sue was watching her, standing by the sand pile, when a lawn mower whirred up behind her, so quickly and so close that she jumped.

'Bill Barry! Aren't you a little old for that sort of thing?'

'Just wanted to wipe that fatuous smile off your face. Who do you suppose would turn fastest in his grave if he could hear Tabs – Mr Gilbert, or Mr Sullivan?'

'They'd both be tickled to death.'

Bill turned to glower at the lawn. 'I don't understand,' he said, 'how it's possible to grow *nothing* but plantain and crab grass. What happens to all the seed I pay for? I'm going to write to –' It was his turn to jump as a blare of music from the back porch drowned out both Tabitha and the hide-and-seekers.

'St Louis Woman,' a voice bellowed towards the distant mountains. 'With her diamond ring –'

'Good Lord,' Bill said. 'Do they still play that old thing?'

'It's an entirely new arrangement,' Sue answered. 'I understand it's got a wonderful passage on the clarinet – or the tuba – or something. Howard explained it to me very carefully.'

Bill shuddered and directed the lawn mower to the farthest reaches of the grounds, but Sue smiled broadly at the back porch. What she wanted to do for Cal had been accomplished.

It hadn't happened all at once, but it had happened much faster than Sue had dared to hope.

This afternoon's bedlam, in fact, had had its beginning a full eight days ago – when Howard Phinney found himself in possession of a new album of records at the precise moment that his gramophone died of overwork. Sue, in consequence, was confronted by a delegation of the

neighbourhood youth, imploring her, as proprietor of
the nearest gramophone, to let them use it.

She agreed and the delegation withdrew to the porch,
where 'Peter and the Wolf' and '*Eine Kleine Nachtmusik*'
were put aside and the 'St Louis Blues' installed.

Cal, sauntering across the field, heard the music.

'Mrs *Barry*!' she called, running across the lawn to the
porch. 'What on earth –'

She flung open the screen door and stopped.

Winnie and Dexter were dancing. Howard was
crouched over the gramophone, pointing out intricate
passages to two other boys, who were strangers to
Cal. Cherry was sitting on the couch swing with
another strange boy, both of them tickling the toes
of the indestructible Cathy, retrieved from the flower
bed.

'Hi, Cal!' Cherry called, over the clarinet solo.
'Howard's got the new Carl Ladshead album, and Mr
Barry said we could play it here.'

Sue, in the kitchen, paused with a half-peeled peach
in her hand. There was a silence. Then Cal said:

'I love Carl Ladshead. I always listen to the Wells
Cheese Hour.'

'You *do*!' Howard exclaimed, rising. 'Did you hear
him last week when he played –'

' "One O'clock Jump"? Yes. That was swell! Have
you got it?'

'No,' Howard said, 'but listen to this.' He took another
record from the album, and once again the welkin rang
with the intricate caterwauling so dear to the lovers of
hot music.

Cal, with no self-consciousness whatever, had joined
the group of worshippers around the gramophone.

When the record was finished the boy sitting beside

Cherry said, 'Hey! You're the girl who was with us when we went hunting for Johnny.

Cal looked at him carefully. 'Oh, yes,' she said, 'I remember you, now. But it was so dark, and you all had on those uniforms – I didn't recognize you for a minute.'

'He's Jack Williams,' Cherry said. 'And those two are Freddie and Frank Blair. You know everybody else – except Cathy. Say hello to Cal, Cathy.'

'Gu-uh!' said Cathy.

'And guh to you, Miss Bonney,' Cal said. Everybody laughed and the concert proceeded.

Sue drew a deep breath. 'Bill was right,' she said to Veazie Ann. 'The minute she got straightened out with her mother she straightened out with everybody else.'

'Looks like it,' said Veazie Ann.

It looked even more like it when Sue went out with Coca-Colas, and Cal made a proposal of her own.

'Mrs Barry,' she said, 'I've got a lot of records at home, and there isn't time to bring them over now, because Dexter and Howard have to go home and do their chores. But I could bring them over tomorrow? You wouldn't mind?'

'Heavens, no!' said the thankful Sue.

That was the beginning.

The next step came a few days later when Cal announced that she was going to the movies with Howard.

'He's really awfully nice,' Cal said, half-apologetically. 'And I know he isn't asking me because of the way I look. He saw me all that night when we were trying to find Johnny and I was filthy. My hair was all over my face. I looked,' she said proudly, 'just *horrible*!'

'Of course he's a nice boy, and I'm sure he asked you because you know so much about jazz. But don't try to look horrible tonight. Wear your lavender linen and your black slippers.'

Cal's face glowed with sudden happiness. 'That's just what Mother said!'

The words were commonplace but Cal's tone was not. Mona Stuart, it seemed, was learning, too.

'Oh, and Mrs Barry,' Cal went on, 'I've never worn any make-up, but all the girls do – just a little. Don't you think I *should*?'

Sue looked at her thoughtfully. It seemed a pity, with that magnificent colour and fine skin, but it was true that even the fourteen-year-olds, nowadays, were allowed – on social occasions – a very little, light pink lipstick. But no rouge or powder. And if there was one thing in the world that Cal needed to do, just now, it was to conform.

'A little lipstick,' Sue told her. 'I've an extra one that I can't use – it's too pink – and it ought to be just right for you.'

'You'd better show me how to put it on,' said the bright-eyed Cal. 'I don't want it all over my face.'

Sue told Bill about it, later. 'I feel like Pygmalion,' she said. 'And you can just take me to the movies this evening. I want to see how it works out.'

'You can't see anything in the movies,' Bill reminded her.

'They'll go to the Sweet Shop afterwards. They always do.'

'Oh, Lord!' Bill moaned. 'Do I have to spend my spare time knee-deep in adolescents?'

'Tonight you do, darling.'

The movie, fortunately, was one that Bill wanted to see, and afterwards Sue lured him to the Sweet Shop. He chose the most obscure booth.

'You can stare at them if you like,' he said, 'but I'm darned if they're going to stare at me.'

'They wouldn't look at you twice,' Sue assured him. 'You're too old.'

It was at that instant that Cal and Howard appeared, and sat down at one of the big tables near the juke box.

Cal looked far from horrible. Her lavender dress suited her perfectly, and she wore, as a stole around her shoulders, the many-coloured scarf. The beautifully patterned material and the tiny bells, however unusual, were somehow right on Cal.

She had not noticed Sue and Bill and was talking gaily to Howard about the movie when the door of the Sweet Shop opened – and Amalie Rand came in.

Sue gave a faint moan of dismay. It was important that Cal's first date should go off well and happily, and there was an unpleasant gleam in Amalie's eye when she saw that Cal was with Howard. Still, Amalie was with an older man – he was at least eighteen – and he looked like someone from the city. There was a chance that Amalie might not be too concerned, for the moment, with rural friends. What really worried Sue was the fact that Amalie was wearing a multi-coloured scarf like Cal's. It was redder, and it had golden bells, but it was unmistakably the work of the same designer, and it did not look right on Amalie, whose commonplace brunette prettiness was unequal to it.

Amalie pounced on Howard. 'Hel*lo* there!' she cried. 'Where've you been? I haven't seen you for ages. This is Mr Carling – Derrick Carling. He's staying at the Bald Trail.' She turned to Cal. 'And this is – er – this is Miss Stuart. I'm so sorry, but I've forgotten your first name.'

Derrick Carling, who had not taken his startled eyes from Cal's face since he had first seen it, stepped forward with enthusiasm. 'How do you *do*!' he exclaimed.

'Sit down everybody,' said Howard. 'There's plenty of room.'

Cal looked disconcerted but there was no sign of her usual stony withdrawal. 'Yes, do sit down,' she said quietly.

Amalie's voice went on through the general scraping of chairs. 'I told Derrick he just *had* to take me to the movies so he could see what a really *quaint* place this is,' she chattered. 'He thought it was a riot, didn't you, Derrick?'

Derrick looked uncomfortable. 'Why, no,' he said. 'It seemed fine to m –'

Amalie interrupted him, speaking across the table to Cal. 'I remember your name now,' she said. 'It's Cal. I guess I forgot it because I never see you anywhere. You don't go out much, do you?'

The venom in her tone communicated itself to the two boys who looked at one another and shifted their feet.

Amalie continued without pause. 'And I hope you don't mind my asking – but how do *you* happen to have one of these?' She touched her scarf.

Cal seemed less annoyed than surprised.

'Why, someone gave it to me,' she said.

'But they're *new*,' Amalie protested. 'My mother sent me this from *Paris*. They were shown at the Clarice opening.' There was real chagrin in her voice.

Cal hesitated, unaccustomed to all this fashionable competition. Then, as she told Sue afterwards, she remembered the girls at school, and their terrific effort to have the latest skirt length, or colour, or gadget, and she felt suddenly warm and comfortable.

'I've had this for over a year,' she said, with just the right note of indifference. 'Mother knows Clarice very well, and Clarice wanted to design a dress for me, after

Mother did her portrait. But Mother wouldn't let her, so Clarice did this for me instead. Afterwards, she asked if I minded if she made some for sale.'

Amalie stared at Cal, completely taken aback, and there was a silence.

'I think that's swell,' said Howard loyally.

'It's an awfully convenient scarf,' Cal went on. 'Clarice showed me how to fold it so that I can wear it on my head. It's quite tricky to get the bells just right. I'll show you, sometime, if you like.'

'No thanks,' said Amalie. 'I like mine the way it is. Derrick, let's run along. The light in this place makes my eyes tired.'

She retreated into the night, dragging the uncomfortable Derrick with her. She did not say good-bye.

'What's eating her?' Howard demanded.

'I don't know,' said Cal dishonestly.

'Well, nuts to her, anyway. Let's dance.' He put a nickel in the juke box.

Bill looked across at Sue. 'Do we have to stay here any longer?' he asked.

'Nope. We can go home. The last dragon has been slaughtered. But you needn't look so superior. You were eavesdropping like mad, and if you ask me, you were just as spellbound as I was.'

Bill rumbled in his throat.

That had been nearly a week ago, and now Cal was as firmly entrenched in Springdale's younger set as if she had lived there all her life. Some afternoons she spent at the Bonneys'; on others they all went swimming; again, as today, they all came to Sue's.

Sue rejoiced in the bedlam.

'How do you stand this?' said a voice from the other side of the sand pile, from which Sue was still watching

Tabitha and listening to the highly individual interpretation of Gilbert and Sullivan.

It was Mona Stuart.

'Stand what?' Sue asked, dodging Johnny, who passed her at a wild gallop.

Mona Stuart made a gesture which encompassed the swing, the lawn, the uproar from the back porch, and even the lawn mower.

'I don't know,' said Sue. 'You get used to it. To tell the truth, I rather like it.'

Mona Stuart looked at her with respect. 'I believe you do. You're a remarkable woman, Mrs Barry. Is my child here?'

'She is – right on the porch with the others. Shall we go and find her?'

'If you think it's all right. I – I wanted to see just what it is that's making her so happy these days. She's like a different child.'

'You know perfectly well what's made her happy,' said Sue bluntly.

Mona Stuart smiled. 'I know the fundamental reason. I'd like to see some of the externals – if you think it's wise.'

'Why not? Come on.'

But as they approached the back porch Mona Stuart began to look alarmed. 'What do I say to them?' she asked nervously.

'Say anything you like. They're just nice kids, and even if they make a noise like a menagerie, they won't bite.'

Sue opened the door and Cal, who had been sitting with Howard, listening, sprang to her feet.

'Mother!' she said.

Howard switched off the gramophone and Mrs Stuart

was confronted by the awe-stricken silence of half a dozen adolescents.

'This is Cherry Bonney,' Cal said. 'And Dexter, and –'

'Oh, go right on playing,' Mrs Stuart said hastily. 'I just came to listen, myself.'

'Why don't you sit down and make yourself comfortable,' Sue advised. 'I'll go and get some fresh tea.'

Mrs Stuart sat down, and Cal settled herself on the floor, leaning shyly but proudly against her mother's knees. Howard, desirous of consolidating his position with Cal, came to talk to her mother.

Sue didn't hear the first awkward beginning. She was just coming out with the tea when Howard discovered what he believed to be a topic of mutual interest.

'I read a book about an artist, once,' he said. 'I guess he was kind of crazy. He cut off his ear and sent it to somebody.'

'Well!' Mona Stuart snapped. 'Don't worry! I'm not going to send anybody an ear of mine!'

Howard stared at her and then, convinced that Cal's mother was the wittiest person he had ever met, he burst into roars of laughter. Between guffaws he repeated what she had said, and in the general merriment Mrs Stuart managed to laugh, too. She seemed rather pleased at being considered a humorist and asked Howard what else he knew about artists.

He described an occasion when the back hill on his father's farm had caught fire, and as he and his father fought desperately to extinguish it, a woman with a sketchbook appeared and drew the scene – which she later said was 'picturesque'. The sound of Mrs Stuart's laughter rose even above Howard's.

'Why,' she demanded abruptly, 'don't you all come

over to my place, sometime, and try out your records on Cal's gramophone?'

Sue took one look at Cal's happy face and slipped around to the front door with the intention of unearthing Bill. There were matters she wished to discuss.

The front door was closed and Sue smiled at the perversity of human nature. In winter the children could never remember to close the door; in summer they closed it religiously.

She opened it – and crashed into somebody who was just about to enter.

'For Pete's sake!' said a familiar voice. 'That was my chin.'

Sue stepped back, rubbing her cheekbone.

'*Kit!*' she exclaimed.

Kit grinned. 'Didn't you get my wire?'

'No. Did you send one?'

'Uh – well – there you have me. I thought I did.' She paused for a moment, listening to the bedlam of sound coming from the yard and the back porch.

'As a matter of fact I was looking for a respectable family named Barry who used to live here – but I see the place has become a third-rate roadhouse.'

'Third rate, nothing! It's a combination of Civic Centre and Youth Hostel – full of good works. Don't you read my letters? Oh, Kit! I'm so glad you're back. Bill was just about to go into mourning for you, too. His association with Miss Landers is not at *all* what it should be.'

'Going to put me up for a week or so?' Kit asked, ignoring Miss Landers.

'I don't know. I'll have to think it over. I like to have good influences around the children. Oh-oh! Tabs has seen you.'

'*Aunt Kit! Aunt Kit!*' Tabitha screamed from the swing and hurled herself out of it to race across the lawn. The twins heard her.

'Aunt Kit!' they shouted, running after Tabitha. They flung themselves upon Kit in a body.

'Heavens!' said Kit presently, standing up with her hat over one ear. 'Anybody interested in presents?'

'WE are! We are! We are!'

'All right,' Kit said. 'Suppose we all go upstairs. I'd like to change before I encounter the jive on the porch. Same room, as usual?'

'Same room,' Sue told her. 'I'll be up in a minute – I've got some news for you. But first I want to find Bill.'

Sue ran downstairs, humming, and went on into the yard. Bill had put away the lawn mower and she found him in the barn, looking into the unused feedbins.

'Hello, darling,' said Sue. 'Kit's back.'

'Thank the Lord! Where is she?'

'Upstairs with the kids.'

'Swell! Listen, Sue – have you seen that ten-pound sack of lime I bought last spring? There's a lot of moss under the north maples.'

'No, I haven't. Bill, I want to talk to you.'

'Go right ahead,' Bill agreed absently. 'Boy! Will I be glad to see the last of that Landers woman; but it does seem to me that I had that sack in here somewhere. I want to lime now, before the autumn rains, so that next year the lawn –'

'BILL BARRY! Never mind your old grass! Nor Miss Landers – nor Kit!'

Bill looked at her in astonishment. 'What's the matter, darling?'

'I've got some things I want to say, and I want to say them right now.'

Bill turned to her with his never-failing concern, and they sat down on the edge of the feedbin. 'Tell Papa,' he said.

Sue did not reply at once. Now that the moment had come she wasn't sure how to begin.

'You know how I hate waste,' she said at last.

'Sure,' said Bill, waiting.

'Well, for a long time I've had an uncomfortable feeling that I'm not doing as much as I ought. I've been wondering if I were wasting myself.'

'*Sue!*'

'No, no! You know what I mean – all that wonderful training – all those years of study – it seemed to me that I was just throwing them away for my own personal happiness.'

'If you'll forgive my being so *un*-high-minded,' Bill said, 'I'd like to point out that it was *my* happiness, too – not to mention the children's!'

'I know that, dear. I've been thinking about it all summer.'

'You're off the beam,' said Bill quietly. 'Most of us could do more than we're doing, but it's a mistake to take on more than you can do well. There are a lot of happy people in this house because you're the kind of person you are, and lead exactly the life you do. You've done enough neighbourhood nursing this summer to last you ten years. You've cured Cal of a serious neurosis into the bargain, and prevented an internationally famous artist from becoming a bewildered and embittered old woman.'

'I couldn't have done it without your help.'

'That's not the point. The point is that you have a talent for people – and your training has developed it. Our children will grow up to be happy, normal, and highly useful – because they have the kind of mother they *should* have.'

Sue rubbed her cheek against his shoulder. 'Thanks,' she said. 'I guess you've straightened me out on that one; but there's something else. Bill – do you wish you had a quieter life?'

'Sure, but I doubt if it would be good for me. Why?'

'Because things are going to be even less quiet in a few months.'

'I don't get it.'

'Shrieks in the night,' Sue explained. 'Two a.m. feedings. The thunder of tiny feet.'

Bill sprang to his feet. 'Do you mean to sit there and tell me –?'

'Well, we've got three children – why not four? There's plenty of room, and there's no point in my stagnating.'

Bill's face was glowing. He caught Sue's hands and pulled her up against his grease-stained shirt. 'Aren't you ever satisfied?' he asked.

'No,' said Sue.